# Rebellion Rising

## Ashleigh Cattermole-Crump

First Edition
Published
Nordic Press
Kindlyckevägen 13
Rimforsa, Sweden.
2022
This is a work of fiction. Similarities to real people,
places, or events
Are entirely coincidental
Rebellion Rising
Ashleigh Cattermole-Crump
978-91-987509-9-7
Cover Design by
C. Marry Hultman through Wombo Art
Illustrations by Wombo Art
Formatted by
C. Marry Hultman
Edited by
Derek Power

# CHAPTER I

News of the crash came in as I set a pitiful dinner on the table, the static from the radio reaching out and pulling my father into his office. From the intermittent signal, I managed to capture a few scraps of words; "ocean craft... down.... distress...no survivors." That was the danger of our island. Jagged rock lay just below the surface of the toxic, algae-laden water snatching up any ill-intentioned intruders. After my father had struggled into his moth-eaten Guard's vest and galloped out the door, I lunged for my stiff, weather-soaked boots, wondering what was out there.

I was halfway down the rickety steps when I saw her. A pile of flesh and seaweed. Sheltered from the storm with only a coat, I glanced around. Deafening rain but no sign of company. I knew I should call for help, alert a guard but a shiver ran down my spine that had nothing to do with the sheets of rain pouring from above. I felt the same twinge of excitement I had on the day that I discovered the mushrooms in our porch planter were hallucinogenic. I froze, unsure which way to turn. My feet, sandy and waterlogged, refused to move and my voice caught in my throat. Checking my father had disappeared into the night, I knelt low and slipped my hands underneath the bedraggled figure and started to pull her up the beach. A thick bag dropped from the girl's arm, and I hoisted it up onto my shoulder, panic setting in.

The water slapped itself against the sand, leaving a soft sizzle in its wake and I could feel my breath coming in shallow gasps. Reaching a handout, I heard the pile of soggy debris and ruddy limbs cough. She shivered and tried to stand, shaking free a bruising of sand and rocks. I caught a glimpse of matted black curls. Best guess, I put her around thirty. Even half-drowned I could see she did not have the Republic-mandated hair length, and her dress of black and purple lace was most definitely not the official green linen of our island's workers. Where had her boat come from? And where were the rest of her crew?

The labs and housing barracks, built high above the beach, stared down at me, harsh and unforgiving. I almost turned back. I would be dead if they knew I helped her. But as I tucked my hands into my apron pocket, my fingers brushed against the old worn photograph that lived in there. An icicle slid down my throat. With another breath, this one full of ice and sand, I placed a hand around the woman and hauled her to her feet. She muttered something thickly in an accent I couldn't understand but she managed to half-walk, half-hop along the beach with me holding most of her weight. I urged her forward. We needed to hurry. I glanced around, found emptiness. I led her to a small, sheltered cave that was impossible to find if you didn't know it was there. As children my brother had shown me the entrance, a place he often hid from our father when he was drinking and violent. Water was seeping into the opening, but the tide was on its way out and I heard an alarm sound from above. Damn! If I took much longer, the beach outside would be filled with Guards, and we would both be hung for treason.

"Stay here. I'll come back," I told the woman, not knowing if she even understood me. I pulled a few pieces of dried seaweed and berries from my apron. I pushed one of the slimy green leaves up to my mouth and ran it along my gums, an old trick my mother had taught me. She said it helped keep lungs from ingesting too many toxins from the salty air. The berries, edible, would give the stranger at least a scrap of energy. And she certainly looked like she needed it.

"Stay as far out of sight as possible," I told her, pushing her gently backwards to where a dry rocky space opened and wrapped my coat around her shoulders. I nodded, propped my lamp against a dry rock. God, I hoped she understood

Not for the first time, I wished that there was a way of contacting someone-anyone-on the outside. Since the failed rebellion two decades earlier, the one that had seen my mother hung for treason, the outer Islands were forced into isolation. A 'safety measure' they told us as children. The Republic needed to force control somehow. A shiver ran through me as I thought about what would happen to me if the guards ever discovered the stranger, but it was quickly replaced by excitement. I had just found a connection to the outside world. As I shook the rain off my coat, a stray drop found the gas lamp that lit our living room, and I heard a hiss as the room was thrown into shadows. Electricity on the outer islands was almost non-existent. We had to make do, and so in the dimness I pulled out the tattered and slightly soggy photograph that lay folded into the hem of my pocket. It was from the early times, pre-rebellion, when I was only a baby. My parents stood in a library. My brother, barely five, held the chubby pile of lace and tuft of orange hair that was the only proof of my existence before The Islands closed themselves off to each other. I certainly had no memory of then, of her, or of the books that once lined the shelves of our home. They were now long gone, a tool of the rebellion.

When my father returned, his thick boots left puddles in the hall.

"Did you find anything?" I called after him, trying to stop my rapidly blinking eyes and my lips that threatened to crack into a smile.

"Aye. Battered mess," he called back. "Ships wrecked; we'll do a deep dive tomorrow. Ain't nobody survived that."

I nodded, my chest pounding. My thoughts wandered to the girl in the cave. I couldn't risk going back now; the flicker of flames from the beach told me that the other Guards had set up watch until reinforcements could be brought in. I imagined her shivering and cold and my heart almost dropped through my soggy boots. I prayed she would make it through the night.

My thin blankets felt scratchy and irritating as I tossed in bed. I could hear the siren in the distance, signalling the changing shift workers. I imagined them, in single lines, trooping back to the barracks where their mandated rations awaited; the perfect number of calories to ensure their productivity. My own stomach turned as I imagined my life if I had been designated as 'unskilled labour'. And I would have been if not for the knack with plants I had inherited from my mother. Adrenaline coursed through me. For the first time in a long while I had found a way to rebel against the Republic that involved more than a stolen cigarette or traded rations.

Slowing my breathing, I slipped a hand under my mattress and found the small envelope of papers that snuggled there, hidden, comforting. Since the Rising, we were the remnants of humanity. The most wretched of us were destined to be Islanders for life, our realities consisting of nothing, but the regimented daily labour enforced upon us since adolescence. My brother had told me stories of what it was like Before. These scraps of paper were the only proof I had that it wasn't always like this. Laying in a kind of half-sleep I waited for the morning. For the reset button.

# CHAPTER II

My delegated work usually took place in the day, my greenhouses boasting a huge range of poisons, medical plants, and the like. The Lab, as it was usually known, was hastily built in the early years following the Rebellion, a desperate attempt to form some sort of food production chain. I'd had crescent moons of dirt underneath my fingers as long as I could remember, most of my time spent at home coaxing shoots and leaves from the soil. When my brother was here, he used to tell me the stories our mother had told him. About the 'Beforetimes'. I hung onto his every word as he described great lakes, mountains, huge swathes of land that rolled on forever. I listened. And I waited. For the mountains and the lakes and the freedom. As I grew, life reminded me; nothing and no one was coming to rescue me. And so, I dreamed of rescuing myself.

"Cutting it fine," the guard outside my laboratory door murmured, tapping his watch as the doors clanged open. As I entered the main grow house, I was disappointed at the lacklustre offering that plants had produced overnight. I already knew the latest cultivation would fall short for the second month running but I still gritted my teeth in annoyance. Last time I had failed to produce enough, I had taken three strikes to the back. The slashes had bled through my dress for a week.

"The nightshades are coming along," my assistant Uma said as she marched out of the humid plastic sheeting that housed the poison-ous cuttings. She too wore the square-necked green linen that indicated our position as obe-dient citizens of the island, but she somehow made it look more like a prison uniform, her deep, constant scowl terrifying even to most of the Guards. I nodded, my mind still on the woman I had left in the cave. Had she survived the night in my pitiful wool coat? I wanted nothing more than to bolt out the door, to scour the cliffs and beaches for her, but I held my-self still, my fingers pinching my thigh skin through my dress as I often did when I felt the panic tingling in my chest.

"Any luck with the muscipula?" I asked, in an attempt to act normally. Uma was at least a foot shorter than me, her squinting eyes re-minding me that the slightest misstep in her presence would ultimately lead me to the stock again. She was not one to bend the rules.

"Not this time, tides have been weak. I've already asked, and they won't push back the deadline, useless bastards. Those guards are useless, did you hear about the shipwreck last night? We could be in danger, and I caught one sleeping just now! Imagine if someone broke in here? You just know it'll be you and me that paid the price," Uma muttered, shaking her head and marching back towards the herb crops.

"The Republic have been asking for extra ginkgo root," she called over her shoulder, and it took all my strength to keep my eyes unrolled and placed firmly in their sockets. *Useless demanding pricks.* Uma raised her eyebrow and shook her head, offering me a small smile. I felt a momentary release from the concern that had bound my throat since the prior evening. Uma had been a friend of my mothers and since her death, Uma had taken me under her wing to a certain degree. She was brisque but I secretly whispered a thank you to the universe every day for putting her in my path and getting me the job in the Lab.

I peered out of my window, coated with a dirty green sheen. The beach was buzzing with activity. Parts of the wrecked boat were being brought ashore and inspected as the black coats of the Guards milled around the rocks. I shivered as I saw the medics every now and then, pulling in bodies. My father was probably down there, he was consistently praised for having the "structure and discipline good soldiers required" and he hated to be left out of anything. Well, anything except family life and sobriety. Since I had turned eighteen I had held onto the spark of rebellion that had thrilled me whenever I avoided his vicious growl or managed to siphon off a few glasses of his whiskey. For the first time in several years, I felt a pang of missing my brother. He always managed to bend the rules to our advantage. My whole childhood, he had been my protector, my only friend. But when he left, I had tucked him into a box, locked it tightly and refused to open the memories of him.

"What are the export numbers?" I called out to Uma who still had not emerged from the forest of crops we had engineered inside the lab.

"We're down on maize and feverfew," she replied. "The nightshade project seems to be on track though."

I sighed. The orders had come down from the top. It seemed like every month the demands on us grew. They wanted more food, more medicines and now...more poisons.

"You!" I heard a voice sound from the doorway. I didn't recognize the voice, so I bowed my head modestly and shuffled over. I knew the process of new Guard arrivals by now.

"Boats here."

The speaker was a large man, tightly bound in a black military suit, the buttons straining against his chest the same way his eyes were protruding from his face as I approached.

"We haven't got the export ready yet...

Sir," I added quickly as his eye twitched.

"That's unfortunate." The man was wearing the same name badge every other guard and citizen was forced to wear. Roland.

My own badge projected my image and name, Valrye, just above the neck of my dress. I saw his eyes linger a little too long and I shifted uncomfortably. His lip was lifted in a sneer as he motioned over one of the old Guards.

"Guard Blackwell, the good lady scientist here tells me that they will not be making the quota this month," the new arrival said. "Remind her of what the punishment for that is?"

Blackwell's face was blushed to the red of the flowers the island had tried desperately to stop from extinction years before. I held my hands tightly together in my apron pocket, avoiding Blackwell's eyes. *Come on, please!* I thought. He had always been kind to me.

"Um," Blackwell began, avoiding my eyes. "Sir, the tides have been low this month. We haven't been able to produce-"

"That was not my question."

The man stepped into my space, his breath warm against my cheek. "Or do you already know?' His finger snaked out and slipped the sleeve of my dress down slightly to reveal the still raw slices they had taken out of my back.

"We just need until tomorrow. The storm…" was all I could manage. I felt as though I was swallowing knives. Words were dangerous. All it would take was this new guard to decide I was being belligerent, and I could be whipped again. His sneer flickered a little and I felt my cheeks burning as he stared down at me. Just as he opened his mouth to reply, another guard burst through the door.

"Storm's coming in faster than we thought!" he called out. "We have to shut it down now."

The man looked me up and down for what felt like a lifetime before eventually dismissing me with a nod. Urgh, he made my skin crawl. Storms weren't uncommon these days, rain and heat were brutal but since storms took out several harvesters a few years back, work shut down now. I took a deep breath, the strikes on my back tingling.

"The seaweed," I practically whispered, my heart thumping.

"Excuse me?" The man's jaw was clenching itself as though he might unhinge it and consume me whole.

"The storm, it'll destroy the seaweed that the tide's just brought in. If you want us to get to quota, I'll need it." I was desperately trying to stop the blush on my face from spreading but despite the chill, my skin was burning.

The guards exchanged looks, before Blackwell finally spoke up. "She's right. The seaweed almost doubles the production numbers."

"I'm not risking one of my men's lives," the new arrival argued, his lip curled in a snarl.

"I can go alone," I quickly whispered. "You can see me from here, where could I go?"

"Fine. Ten minutes." The new guard jerked his head back towards the door. "And if you're not back by then, we'll leave you out for the storm."

I nodded a thanks and retied my apron, making sure the photograph was safe from the rain.

# CHAPTER III

rushed down the awkward stony pathway to the beach. The guards watched my every move from above. Rain was beginning to fall, and I could smell the sulphur that storms always brought in. I needed to hurry. The stink of seaweed reached me, and my fingers tangled through the green clumps and shoved them into my pocket. There were only a few feet of beach that weren't visible from the lab. I flitted across the wet sand, my shoes almost sucked off my feet, and I cursed myself for forgetting to change into my boots. I moved to and fro before gradually allowing myself to slip out of sight. I didn't have long.

At the back of the cave, dampness radiated off the slick stone. My heart vibrated against my ribs. Was she still in here? I crept further and further back. A clack of stone on stone made me jump. I let out a breath. *Thank God.* The woman was alive. Barely. As I waited for my heart to stop pounding, the half-cooked remnants of a plan swirling in my brain-she stood shivering and pale against the back wall of the cave.

"It's ok," I whispered, looking around. "Are you ok?"

I could see the clothing that hung off her frame was weighing her down. Her brows folded when she saw me, and her shoulders hunched. The terror in her eyes was clear even in the darkness. I could almost hear a ticking clock counting down, and I knew I didn't have much time. I motioned to the girl, and we crept back to the beach. The lab looming down on us.

"I have to go," I said to the girl, shielding my eyes from the rain that felt oddly warm. I pointed up at the lab and then at the incoming thunderclouds. "Once the lights up there go out, follow that pathway, until you see a house with a black door."

Her eyes burned into mine. I felt the desperation steaming from her as I swallowed hard. *Come on, just tell me you understand!* As I turned to head back to the lab, I heard her speak.

"Thank you."

As Uma led the line of bow-headed women back to the housing units, I tried to inconspicuously search the dark forest for the stranger. She was out there somewhere, probably slipping around in the muddy darkness. But I could not see anything in the dim. The Guards followed along behind us, and I felt my heart stop as a radio crackled.

"Shift Guard, come in."

"Shift guard here. Over"

"A stranger has been spotted on the beach. All Guards are to report to base after citizen drop off. Over."

I Blackwell grumbled. My heart was in my throat. I tried to plaster an innocent look across my face as Roland was suddenly upon me, his hot breath on my neck. I froze. He fingered the baton on his belt. It felt like an eternity before he turned away.

"Shoot on sight," he said into his radio, eyes boring into mine. I dropped my gaze to the soggy ground, tried to hide my rising panic.

Back in the house, still shaking, there was no sign of the woman. A scattering of papers lay on the table. The Heralds--a thin newspaper dubbed the 'propaganda press' -- featured a smiling face. Well, at least someone's glad to be alive, I thought. Not a word printed inside was truthful, we weren't allowed to know about citizens of the other islands. For our own safety, the Republic said. I could see Roland squinting at me through the window, so I picked up the paper, thumbing through it to look interested in a spread about the *'Wonderful Collections on Coal Island'*. I prayed he couldn't see my hands shaking.

Breathe.

Every muscle in my body clenched.

Stay Calm.

I forced myself to relax, no matter how much I wanted to find the castaway. If she had even made it this far. *What if she hadn't?* A swoop of guilt settled into my stomach. I had sent her through the forest. Straight into the hands of the Guards who knew she was here now. But what choice did I have? I tried to reason with myself. If I had left, her she would have been swept away by the tides or caught hypothermia before she was captured. Who knows, that might have been preferable.

As a child, I had seen people punished, publicly, for their crimes. Hung in the street, drowned, sent out into the water without resources. When I was 12, a woman tried to escape the island by raft and was hung in the centre of the barracks for insubordination. I still remembered the twitching brown leather boots swinging limply. Afterwards, I had rushed behind a shed to vomit, and I heard my father's jeering in my ears. The solution had been to divide the men and women, leaving the women here as workers and the men shipped off to train elsewhere. They were never heard from again. That was the beginning of my complete and utter contempt for the faceless 'leaders' whose boot stood firmly on our proverbial necks. So, if an opportunity presented itself to mess with their rules, I was damn sure going to take it.

There was no movement out the kitchen window, nothing but the beating of raindrops.

She hadn't made it. I distracted myself pruning the herbs that sat limply in the garden. The sage was bruised and let off a mouldy smell, but it was better than the scent of rotting cabbage and stale alcohol. Bootsteps clomped down the stairs, and my father appeared, brushing his hair out of his eyes. Fuck! Why was he here? If he saw the woman, I couldn't imagine he would show much mercy.

"I thought you were on shift?" I stuttered and he didn't look at me as he answered.

"On my way. Crash has been the focus all day."

I nodded, swallowing so loudly he must surely have heard it.

"Have you found the missing woman?"

His eyes slowly ran over me. "How'd you know it was a woman?" he asked, and I felt my breath catch.

"The girls at the lab are saying it, is all."

My father grunted at me, collecting his coat from the back of a chair and lingered by the door, rolling a cigarette. He looked at me for a few seconds then bowed his head. *Come on, just go!* I thought, trying to coax him out the door. Eventually he wandered slowly out into the rain, striking a match against his tobacco.

Before my mind could race through all the horrible places the woman could have fallen to her death, I heard a crash from somewhere behind me. I spun around to see her, still-damp and shivering. I whipped a blanket off the back of a chair and wrapped it around her shoulders. I had a spare linen shift that had begun to fall apart. I tied it around the stranger's body, feeling her ribs jutting from her thin frame and soliciting a wince when I pressed too hard on a bruise. She collapsed onto the tatty chair that groaned when it was sat in.

"Are you ok?" I finally asked, my heart beginning to settle.

She nodded. When she spoke, it was in a hoarse voice. "Have you found anyone else?"

I shook my head. "No. I'm sorry. My father said there were no other survivors. But they saw you, and they're searching. We can hide you here until things settle down, but I... I have no idea how to get you off this island," I finished.

I would have been lying if I said I never thought about it. About how to escape. I spent many an afternoon in my lab daydreaming of the tiny, scalloped boat that would carry me from this prison and on to a whole world of possibilities. But as I grew up and scraps of news came in from the rest of the world, I quickly shelved any thoughts of leaving. There was nothing better out there. Nowhere to go.

"I will make my own way; I will not put you in danger. Thank you for saving me." She tried to push herself up to her feet but cried out in pain.

"No, it's not safe out there. You need to rest. We'll come up with a plan once you've slept," I said, surprising myself at my forcefulness.

I led her upstairs, pulling the string that opened the attic door. A set of stairs slipped down to meet us, and we clambered up to a cluttered room full of old fabric, broken equipment and an assortment of gardening tools. My mother's. I had forgotten they were up here. I made enough space to lay down several layers of blankets. It wouldn't be comfortable, but it would be better than nothing. The woman lay down gratefully, her eyes still not leaving mine. Apparently deciding I could be trusted; she closed her eyes.

"Kimbr," she said, hoisting a few layers over her body. "My name is Kimbr."

Feeling the prickle in my shoulder again I felt a rush of pleasure at making the guards' lives difficult.

"Sleep now," I told Kimbr. "We'll think of a plan in the morning."

Just as I was about to climb back down the ladder, a creak sounded from downstairs, and I felt a terror rising in my belly.

"Wait here. Stay quiet."

felt a terror rising in my belly.

"Wait here. Stay quiet."

# CHAPTER IV

My mouth way dry as I climbed back down the tiny ladder. I didn't know what I expected. A team of armed guards maybe? A guard come to drag me to the stocks for treason?

"Well, well, look what the cat dragged in!" A woman stood in the doorway dressed in a thick rustling yellow jacket, her hair sopping wet as she shimmied herself from her clothes. Relief flooded through my body. Mae. My childhood friend who now ran boats between our island and the neighbouring ports, had arrived for the collection just in time to beat the storm. I felt a relief wash through me when she smiled, a tingle that I wasn't sure I liked. Mae pecked me on the cheek as she headed for the kitchen.

"I didn't see you arrive. What've you brought me?" I asked Mae, a sly grin spreading across my face. My breath quickened and I felt the blood rush to my face as she hugged me.

"What, you mean this rag ain't good enough for ya?" She asked, voice dripping with disgust as she crumpled one of the Heralds that sat on the table. She slipped a small envelope out of her jacket pocket and placed it in my hand. It was paper, scrawled with words, a few newspaper clippings from the Beforetimes pressed between pieces of glass. I smiled, looking forward to adding it to the collection of words I kept under my mattress. I gathered the words of others, their thoughts, dreams, shopping lists. It wasn't the same as reading a book, but it was as close as I could get these days. My own small act of rebellion.

"So, word on the waterways is that ship-wreck was Navigators."

My heart rocketed to my throat. How had I not put that together? Navigators were danger-ous, they had no home, no country. They were the women ousted from society for lack of productive value, who were out only for them-selves. They survived by smuggling and trad-ing with anyone they could. When Mae and I had been caught smoking stolen cigarettes on my 18th birthday, my father had forced us to watch the execution of a Navigator. Tied to a stake and left to drown as the tide came in, I recalled the woman's stoic, bruised face, refus-ing to cry out until the water swirled over her head and the bubbles of her breath dissipated into nothingness.

"My father...he's in charge of the recov-ery"

"Mmmm. And where is the good general?" she asked, a sliver of hatred in her voice.

"On patrol tonight. He won't be back until the morning at the earliest."

I dithered for a moment as Mae stuffed a limp cabbage roll into her mouth, wiping her lips on the back of her hand. I could always trust her. I hoped.

"I found her," I whispered.

To her credit, Mae barely reacted. "What? Who?"

"The escapee." I offered a terrified grin, my nerves frayed to shreds.

"Where?" Mae snapped her head around, her eyes glistening with a mixture of horror and excitement.

"On the beach last night. She's upstairs now, I need a distraction. If they find her..."

"Valrye! She might be dangerous!"

As soon as the words left her mouth, the door behind her crashed open, and several guards spilled into the kitchen, all holding a variety of weapons. We were roughly pushed aside as they spread through the house. Bringing up the rear was Roland, who grinned as he entered, getting a little too close for my liking.

"Searching for the intruder," he said as he whipped past us. "You know how it is, best to catch these people before they can cause trouble."

My head jerked back and forward as I watched the guards turn over everything in the sparsely furnished house.

"We must stop them! If they look in the attic, we're all dead!" I whispered, backing up until I knocked into the wall.

"What exactly do you expect to find in the kitchen cupboards? "Mae said, shooting me a look of faux disappointment and a wink. "There's not even any food in there, might you want to go and sort that out instead of invading people's homes?"

The guard looked surprised that someone dared speak back to him but before he could answer Roland appeared again in the doorway.

"I hope the two of you aren't impeding our search," he grunted, rounding on us. I knew to keep my mouth shut by now, but Mae still hadn't figured out what was good for her. It was part of what made me tremble whenever she was around.

"A search for what? Some bloody manners?"

Without warning, his baton swung heavily. A crack as it caught Mae's knee, her body collapsed to the ground. I stepped back, heart hammering, hands up. *Shit*! Before I could say a word, the guard drew his hand back and it landed square in my chest, forcing the breath from my lungs. Pain shot through my ribs, and I gasped. I went down, the cold floor rising to meet me. Standing over us, Roland looked around.

"We'll be on our way then. Don't get comfortable, I get the feeling I'll be seeing you again real soon."

After the guards' lamps disappeared down

the cliff, I allowed the oxygen to suck back into my chest.

"Jesus, what an asshole," Mae muttered. "I heard the Republic was sending some har-dasses to the islands to ensure we're all behaving. You seem to have made an impression on him."

# CHAPTER V

Mae watched the last of the guards retreat to the station. Satisfied we were alone again, she turned to me and hissed.

"My god, girl, what do you think you're doing? You're playing with fire here. Didn't know you had it in you."

Still, I could tell she was impressed. She'd always been more adventurous than me, I usually stuck to brooding and small aggressions. Mae had once thrown petrified horse poo at a guard battalion. That was what sent her to courier duty. Her familiar smile made me judder a little inside as she knocked the rain off her boots and hobbled up the stairs to shake off the pain from the bat. As we passed my bedroom, I saw they had torn the place apart, and I gasped seeing a wooden horse smashed to kindling on the floor. It had been my brothers as a child, one of the only things left I had of him.

I shivered a little as I thought of my brother for the second time that day. It had been many years since I had seen him sail away to join the training camp for Guards, he vowed never to return while my father still drew breath. And so far, he had kept his promise. My thoughts returned to the girl upstairs and I hurried towards the attic door. A part of me wished I had been caught. I had no idea how to rebel against anything this big, this close. The longer this continued, the more trouble I would be in.

Apparently, Mae did not share my concerns. She bounded ahead of me and swung the door to the attic open. I peered around, sure Kimbr must have escaped amid the chaos but seeing me, she crept out from behind a stack of boxes. Mae stood back and looked her up and down before turning to me, impressed.

"I cannot believe you!" She nudged me on the arm. "Big step up from those times we use to set fires in the guards booth."

I blushed, feeling a flutter at her approval. Shaking myself, I spoke again as Mae's hand brushed against mine.

"Mae, this is Kimbr."

Kimbr narrowed her eyes for a minute before relaxing back onto the makeshift bed, clutching at her injured ribs. The two eyed each other, awkwardly, then Mae burst into a grin. She shook her head, clearly in as much shock as I was.

"Are you a navigator?" I blurted out, unintentionally loud.

She looked surprised but smiled and nodded. "Is that so bad?"

I flinched as Mae dragged an old crate over to sit on, the scraping of the wood on wood screeched like fingernails on glass.

"I can get you something for the pain," I offered but she waved me away.

"How did you get here?" Mae asked, her eyes lit with excitement.

"We were bringing books to the resistance," she replied, her voice strained.

"The resistance? Here? I don't think so.

Kimbr nodded like I was an idiot. "The sisterhood? The dissenters? The rebel group that operates from a base here on this island?"

I shook my head in disbelief. "Here? Are you sure?"

"Pretty positive, considering I've made this trip half a dozen times. Bloody seaweed got caught on our stern this time, smoked out the engine."

I sat back, stunned. Mae however, quivered with excitement.

"I knew it! I knew not everyone wants this

Kumbaya, lets-all-work-for-the-good-of-the-republic bullshit."

Deep down, I must have known it too. The other women on the island barely spoke to me, I was an outcast as the daughter of a Guard. It used to bother me, but as I grew older, I found other interests to pass the time. Now I wondered; I had always assumed they just didn't like me, but had they been hiding something? We were taught from a young age that Navigators were dangerous and deadly, but the woman in front of me…I couldn't tell if she was either. Biting the inside of my lip until I tasted the bitter salty blood as I realized; It was no longer the guards I was defying; it was the Republic itself. And that thrilled me.

"So which Island are you from?" I asked Kimbr, curiosity getting the better of me.

"I'm not from anywhere," she replied, her face darkening. I shuddered, sorry I asked, but she continued. "I was born on the Waste Island, ran when I was barely a teenager. It was that or go to the breeding colony they lovingly call 'Mother Island'. Been with the Navs ever since."

I nodded. Flora Island was a prison but it what if it was the best of the worst? There were islands that mined coal, that bred animals, that took and buried the dead. The ones who had the babies. I had no idea what they were like; Isolation was our collective punishment after the failed rebellion. I usually tried my best not to imagine what they are like or which one my brother might have ended up on.

"What's it like out there?"

Kimbr's face hardened for a second, shaking herself. "It's a mess. I…always thought I knew what was out there, but every time we sailed, we found something worse than the last."

My stomach dropped. "There's nothing out there?"

"Not that I've found, but I heard about a place…a place that's not like this," Kimra said, her voice cracking and I gripped onto her words. I knew it.

"Apparently, there are a few Navs who made it to an Island in the South Pacific. It was always colder there, so it wasn't as affected. It's still cut off; they all fend for themselves. Far as I know the Republic don't even know about it. Or if they do, they're keeping it very quiet."

Beside me, Mae was practically bursting with excitement, and I smiled. Her laugh was one of my favourite sounds in the world.

Kimbr pointed at the large vinyl bag that she had strung around her waist when I found her. As she opened it, a small leak of water sprung to the floor. I peered at the contents, letting out an audible gasp. The mixture of toxic seawater and soggy papers had combined into an intriguing aroma, and I felt myself pulled towards the bag, clutching for the first time in many years a book. A proper, bound in leather book, with the words of souls long lost. Mae let out a snort as my eyes widened at my reaction to my treasure and Kimbr reached inside the bag, flipped open a book and shook out the contents that had been slipped between the back cover. Several tightly rolled cigarettes and an envelope fell out. Kimbr scooped them up and tucked safely inside her pocket. Removing another few books revealed several glass bottles of a strong-smelling liquid and two thin knives. The thrill of the discovery quickly fell away.

"These can't be here!" The words felt sticky in my throat. "If anyone finds these…"

Kimbr nodded. "I know, the Sisterhood are waiting for them. I just need to get them passed on. I promise, it won't come back on you."

"There's no way. There are guards everywhere," Mae pointed out. "Wait until morning."

"I can't. My contact is meeting me tonight. If I don't show up, I don't get paid," Kimbr winced. I shook my head, peering out of the dusty window at the Guard's lamps that continued to bob through the forest. I knew I should let her go alone. Let her trade the goods for her payment but she could barely move, and I couldn't deny the spark of curiosity that had ignited itself somewhere deep in my chest. I sighed, exhaustion trying to pull me into sleep. Apparently, my night was not yet over.

Supported between myself and Mae, Kimbr managed to hobble out the door and together we ducked into the darkness. The two followed along as I tried to guide us through the Guards to the meeting point. I could barely see a foot in front of me. I had only ever been to the other side of the island a few times, usually with my father who, when I was a teenager, didn't trust me at home alone. Which was fair, I had once concocted a mixture of gin and herbs that saw me sitting on the roof. At midnight. Naked.

"What if we don't make it in time?" I whispered as the three of us crouched in a muddy puddle. We needed a break in the Guards to run the length of the open field that sat before us. Kimbr didn't answer, instead pushing herself to a stand.

"Quick, before the next rotation comes around!"

We half-crawled, half-ran through knee-high grass and mud to a part of the island I had never set foot on before. The footsteps of the guards had died out now, the lights disappeared into the depths below us. I squinted, barely able to see anything through the drizzly moonlight but Kimbr seemingly knew where she was going. We neared what appeared to be a collapsed building, and a flash of light hit us in the eyes. Thinking it was a guard, my heart began to pound but Kimbr stood as tall as she could and waved her arms. She was met by a clunk and footsteps.

"Where's Adria?" Kimbr demanded as the source of the light revealed itself. Two figures, dressed completely in black. And they were not pleased. As we were all shoved into the building, the bag falling to the floor, I saw we were in an old barn building. There was a door carved into the floor and one of the black-clothed women opened it and another emerged.

"What the hell is this?" Kimbr's toughness began to sink into exhaustion, and I could see her pale face, straining as she spoke.

"I should ask you the same thing. You're bringing these people to us with the island crawling with guards? What were you thinking? If we get caught, we're all dead. You know that, I assume, not that it matters to you."

"I got the delivery here, didn't I? Just give me the money and we'll get out of here."

Adria shook her head, baring her teeth.

"Not a chance. I am not risking our whole operation for this. You all need to leave. Now."

I squinted in the half-dark, desperately try-ing to remember where I had seen Adria be-fore. She must have been one of the crop girls, the new arrivals from another island. They had only been here a few months.

"You can't do that! I brought these here, risked my own neck. My whole crew were smashed against the rocks, and now you're not going to pay me?"

"All you've brought me is more attention. What do you think those Guards are doing right now? Trying to figure out why Navigators tried to land here, who their network is. And I'll be fucked if we go down because you were careless!"

Kimbr snarled and I saw her arm raise, but I managed to grab her hand before she could punch Adria in the face.

"What if I can get you some more information?" I looked around wildly, my shaking hands clasped onto a nearby banister to steady myself. My brain as whirring from the fact there was a rebellion happening right under my nose. And I sure as hell wasn't going to give up so easily. "Please. My father is a Guard, I can find out things!" I had no idea where the voice had come from, I had never spoken a word of dissent or displeasure to anyone except Mae. Now, suddenly I found myself in the middle of a contraband exchange, offering to risk my neck for a woman I didn't know. Somehow, it made me feel more alive than I had in many years.

"Yes, I know who you are." Adria looked me up and down. "We can't do this here. Or now. You need to get gone. We can talk once the heat dies down."

Before any of us could argue, she had once again hauled the trapdoor open and disappeared into the ground.

As midnight came and went, we traipsed back across the island, the return journey seemingly endless. Back at the house, Kimbr drifted off to sleep on her pile of blankets in the attic and Mae collapsed in exhaustion in the living room. I lay awake, thunder drilling into my skull, the sound of Guards' boots outside eventually disappeared into the night. I felt a hollowness I had never felt before. I had tried so desperately to fill my questioning brain with small scraps of knowledge, the small rebellions, but the thrill that had raced through me over the last few hours had been something else entirely. And now, I wasn't sure how I would ever go back to the meek, quietness of my life.

# CHAPTER VI

After the storm passed, we were allowed back to work. The croppers, the gatherers, the packers headed to the fields, their next twelve hours to be spent bent-backed, their calloused hands and blistering skin repetitively working the never-ending turntable of tasks. The sage-green robes that we all wore melted the procession into the trees that split the island. Once they had disappeared, the transport guards arrived to take us to the labs. The same as always. When my mother had groomed me to follow her path, I had no idea the monotony and the exhaustion that would come from working in an enclosed glass room. At least it's not the fields, I reminded myself. Uma and three others who had been placed on lab duty stood shivering under a veranda.

"Best hope the storm didn't do too much damage. Ain't got no time to be flaffing around clearing up the mess like last time," Uma grumbled as we waited for our escort. I found her gravelly voice oddly comforting, a calmness in a sea of the craziness of the last few days. The doors swung open, and I noticed Roland leading two other sheepish looking men towards us.

"Production is down. You are not reaching quotas," his voice was somehow too loud yet barely audible at the same time. "That stops now. You'll be working until the quotas are filled." His hand sat on his weapon, eyes narrowing in on my own. "The cargo boat leaves at six tomorrow, best hope you're done by then. I'd hate to have to *deal* with this," he said, voice dropping to a whisper. I shivered as the wind blew down my neck.

Once alone in the Lab, I picked a piece of black shade and rubbed it on my top lip, the scent of peppermint offering a boost of energy to my brain, then blessed nothingness. At least for a few minutes, before I was hauled back to reality with the clanging of a falling plant pot. I could just see the edges of the fields where I imagined the back-breaking labour the others must surely be doing, and I felt a pang of guilt. I was here in a lab while others picked thistle weed and food crops in the constantly thinning oxygen. Every week, the crop girls decreased in number. I heard that the ones that dropped dead on the job were left for fertiliser, but Uma told me that was just a rumour they spread to keep us in line. There were a lot of those. A boat would arrive in darkness every few months with their replacements and more than once I dreamed of somehow slipping between the trees and up onto the deck.

Watching through the window as boxes of medicines, jars of toxins, and crates of plants were carted down the steep cliff to Mae's waiting boat, I felt a flutter of thrill in my belly. I squeezed the sides of my arms and shivered a little. It was happening. *Just stay the course, Mae.* "Come on!" I hadn't meant to speak aloud but I was still alone. The guards seemed to move mind-numbingly slow, stopping for a chat or to shake the sand from their boots. The goods were loaded, the boat was ready. So why wasn't it moving? I craned my neck even further. Something was wrong.

"I can't believe we made that run," Uma said from behind me, fanning her face with a half-dead palm frond. "Hopefully that keeps that arsehole off our backs."

"Mmm," I agreed. "Hopefully."

I stood staring at the boat that bobbed on the water, the excitement rising inside me with each turn of the wave. After years of planning and wishing and hoping for a way to get back at the faceless-bureaucracy, I had raised a metaphorical middle-finger to the Republic. I was helping the enemy.

We had timed it perfectly. The guards would add the quotas to the boat and dressed in a black coat of my fathers', Kimbr would slip in between them and onto the boat. I felt proud, a strange feeling I had to admit, but one I liked. A glance out the window at the water whipped that away. Roland. He was marching towards the boat. I saw the edge of the forest where Mae was supposed to meet Kimbr. Three guards stood at the base, looking the other way but Roland marched right past them. As if he knew something, he strode right into the forest, emerging a few seconds later, his hand firmly gripping Mae's upper arm. He led her onto the boat and disappeared below deck. The buzz of excitement that had shivered across me was replaced by a spine-chilling fear as I watched.

Eventually Roland returned to the beach. Me from above and him from the beach, we both watched as the boat sailed away. The cargo I had hoped to be onboard was still loose on the island somewhere. And she had no reason to keep my secrets if she was captured.

# CHAPTER VII

It always felt lonely without Mae. Every time she left, I felt myself break a little bit more. Since my brother had left, she was my only friend. When she was relegated to courier duty because of the small fire in the guard's quarters, I had never felt so alone. And now Kimbr had disappeared as well, maybe not even alive. I sighed, realising I had only the whisky-scented shadow of my rapidly crumbling father for company.

I sat upstairs waiting and staring in amazement at the books. Real, proper books like they had before the world drowned. At least they were a distraction from the thick worry that had settled into me as I wondered where Kimbr was. She was tangible evidence that not everyone bowed down to the Republic, and I had become strangely attached to her over the few hours we had been together.

The slashes in my shoulders ached a little as I thought of what might happen if my father ever found the books. He had accepted his place in this society, he had flourished. He stood by every rule the Republic sent out, every man in it. If his daughter was caught missing quota, and needed to be punished, so be it. He would even oversee the lashings himself. If his only son left on the eve of his 18th birthday and never returned, well what was he to do?

His large form was stooped over the table, knees jiggling. He was sober-ish at least. He ignored me when I walked in, jerking an elbow at the pile of wrapped boxes on the table.

"Rations are here," he croaked. "Should keep you going for a while."

"Great. Do you…do you want some dinner?" I hoped my voice was steadier than it sounded. I couldn't tip him off.

"Nah, not tonight." The chair scraped and he headed upstairs. Half-way up, he stopped and looked back at me. I thought he was going to say something, but he just grunted and continued. I never minded being alone. I ate alone, worked alone, slept alone. But since Kimbr and Mae had so nearly escaped, I felt a kind of hollow emptiness that I hadn't felt since my brother left. I distracted myself with cleaning. Making my way through the living room, the kitchen, the bathroom, all of it seemed darker, colder somehow. I felt a strange warmth at the possibility Kimbr was on her way back. It made me useful to someone. Trying to ignore the feelings of guilt, I turned back to the stairs, beckoned by the books left behind.

I knew from the thick coughing that soon emerged from my father's room that he was smoking a cigar. And if he was smoking, he was also drinking. If he was drinking, I wouldn't see him until morning. I settled into a pile of pillows and reached out for a book I had tucked into a pillowcase and hid under the pot plants. Kimbr's books were unlike anything I had ever seen. They held ideas, thoughts, loves, dreams from people that lived in the Beforetimes. Who really, truly lived? The first book had no title, no distinguishing marks but when I opened the front cover an image of a single flower adorned the first page. I inadvertently let out a gasp as I turned the pages. Loopy letters had been hastily scrawled across one of the pages: *My Darling Clementine, I hope this finds your garden blooming. Everything I learnt about the earth, I learnt from here. Love Always, mum.* The book had been read many times, corners were folded over, pen marks scribbled in the margins. It was a gardening bible. Looking at the cover, it was published in 2029, just a few years before the Great Rising had been triggered. Flicking through pages, I found the section on roses and smiled to myself. I imagined how they would smell, how the velvet of their petals would feel against my fingers.

I read through the evening until my candle burnt to the wick and the room was lit only by the pale moonlight. I devoured words from doctors, stanzas by poets, fiction that told of the green farms of a hundred years ago and at the very bottom of the pile, a collection of essays about how to stop climate change irreversibly damaging the planet. Guess that one came a bit too late. The words soothed me, the knowledge I was finally connected to something else, to someone else, made me feel a little faint. Yet I remained agitated, waiting for news of Kimbr. It was almost midnight before she appeared at the door again, an annoyed look on her face and a gash on her leg dripping blood onto the leaves. I felt my chest constrict and I sucked in a breath before racing back downstairs.

"What happened?" I asked, once in the safety of the attic.

"Bloody Guards. That big bloke, the one who's a real prick, you know…"

I knew. "Roland."

"He set up a patrol of the forest, right where I was supposed to meet Mae. He found her waiting and insisted he escort her to the boat. She had no choice, she had to go with him. And I'll be damned if he didn't watch that boat every second until she pulled away." I sighed. It had been a poor plan; I should have known it wouldn't work.

"We can try again. Next time Mae arrives." I knew the possibility of keeping our secret lessened every day the girl stayed here.

"I don't have time for that. And neither do you. If they catch me here…" she trained off. I knew exactly what would happen. The stripes on my back would be the least of my worries.

Kimbr paced as best she could with her injured leg which she refused to let me bandage.

"The Sisterhood," she replied eventually with a shake of her head.

"Oh yes, because they were so welcoming last time."

"Yeah, but what else can we do? I figure if I can give them something they want then they'll have to help us."

"What do they want, though?"

"Information."

I took a deep breath. That was the most valuable thing on the islands. Unfortunately, it was the most difficult thing to come by. But it was also the only ticket I had to get Kimbr, maybe even myself off this island. Until that moment, I hadn't dare hope that this all might mean freedom. I simply had to focus on one thing at a time. Kimbr. Mae. Uma. They were all in danger, but maybe…I shook myself a little. I tried not to think of myself, but I couldn't help it. This might be my only chance of escape.

The next morning, bolstered by the thrill of dissention and the questions Kimbr had brought with her, I ran down the stairs, a genuine smile on my face for the first time in a while. My father sat, looking rather dishevelled, at the kitchen table. He rarely looked at me, but when he did, I could see it stir something inside him. I knew he saw my mother's brown eyes in my own. And so, I was revered with a cross between nostalgia and hatred. I tried to hide the bags under my eyes and the newfound discomfort that had buried itself in the pit of my belly.

"Morning," I said cheerily, not expecting a reply.

"I hear you made quota, even after the storm," he spoke gruffly, not looking at me. "That's…good."

I was too surprised to answer and before I could stammer out a thank you, he had risen and headed for the door. That was strange, he had never taken an interest in my work before.

As I walked to the shift meeting point, I wondered how had I lived so many years believing the Island had to be my whole world? I had always known there were others, sure, but the realisation that on those islands there were thousands of people living without any kind of knowledge of history, the true history of our people…It had hit me harder than I ever thought it could. But they were out there, probably thinking the same thing. Nevertheless, I had to shake it off. The Lab awaited.

# CHAPTER VIII

Roland was strolling up and down the thin strip of glass floor that held the Lab above the forest. Through the grimy and dusty floor, the overgrowth and vines were piled, pressing against the walls of the tunnel that must once had overlooked a beautiful cityscape. I felt a flicker of nausea, but before the Guards took up their station, I approached the cabinet that held records that had been saved from the Rising. They were piled haphazardly, locked away behind glass. I hadn't ever paid much attention to it before. My father had shown my what was in there once, probably an attempt to stop me from trying to break into it.

I glanced around. I was alone, but I knew I didn't have more than a few seconds. I wondered vaguely why the Guards were running behind, but I focused in on my prize. Information. Useful information? Maybe. The lock, rarely used, had rusted and it only took a small jiggle with a box-cutter to jimmy it open. I listened for incoming guards. Silence. The papers appeared to be written in other languages, a few scribbles here and there. It occurred to me, as my throat dried and I swallowed razors, that any useful information would have been taken long ago. This was essentially a museum exhibit. Slipping a few of the papers into my apron, I didn't have time to second-guess myself before the doors behind me opened.

Roland strolled towards me, hands in his pockets as though the evening before he hadn't placed those hands on me. I turned to my station and picked up a seedling, trying to force my hands to remain steady.

"Not today. I've got another job for you."

My teeth gritted; my heart felt as though I might collapse from stress, but I kept my head bowed in what I hoped was a show of humility.

"What kind of job?"

"Move it," was all he said by way of an answer, and I felt his hot, thick hand on the small of my back. He shoved me so hard I stumbled, and he jerked his head towards the door. He stalked ahead, and I hurried to keep up. We passed the greenhouses, the harvest rooms, the Guards station and just as I thought he was going to march us right outside again, he took a sharp left turn. I was suddenly faced with a thick metal door that I had never seen open. Uma told me that it was where they kept the plants that had been genetically engineered to grow without sunlight or water. Unfortunately, my predecessor hadn't quite figured out how to make them stop growing and it was shut away before it could take over the whole island. Roland slipped a key into the lock, and I heard the scrape of rusted metal as he shoved a shoulder against the door.

The stench of death and rotting organics unfurled from inside and I gagged, taking a step back. Roland, not one to ask twice gripped my arm, his fingers digging in as he propelled me forward into the room. As my eyes adjusted to the darkness, I could see there were indeed huge, towering branches hanging above, their tendrils reaching down in a blind grab for my scruffy hair. Roland walked silently ahead, and I asked myself if he was leading me to an 'accident', where I might never be seen again. In the middle of the overgrown room, his hand reached inside his pocket, and he flicked out a matchbox. Striking one, he lit a nearby lamp and the room was suddenly eye-stingingly bright. I couldn't stop the gasp that creaked in my throat from escaping.

"What is this place?" I asked, refusing to blink in case it all disappeared. There were branches that had grown to the shape of the room, leaves larger than my head and directly ahead, the most beautiful collection of roses I had ever seen.

Flowers were largely extinct now. The limited resources had meant hard decisions in the early years. The botanists and labourers of the island had been forced to focus on food crops, oxygen production and medical plants. The frivolity of plants that had no direct bene-fit to the community was discarded years ago. And yet here in front of me were blooms, pet-als dripping with dew and thorns forcing their way through the bushy surroundings. Roland was watching me, his eyes narrowed as though he wished he were anywhere else.

"The Republic wants these regenerated," was all he said by way of explanation.

"Why?" I asked, my heart fluttering. May-be I was still on edge from the evening's excitement, but I had never seen even a scrap of something beautiful from The Island. Was this it?

"That's not really any of your business, is it?" Roland scowled, his irritation returning. He disappeared into the overgrowth for a moment, soon returning with a large bucket filled with rusted garden tools. I momentarily considered picking up the bent trowel and burying it in his neck. Instead, I offered a smile that probably looked more like a grimace and thanked him.

"You have until the next boat arrives to make some progress, otherwise I'm afraid you might find yourself…unnecessary."

I allowed my fingers to reach out and brush against the bruised velvet petals. I had never touched anything so soft. Most of the plants I worked with were bred to excessive usefulness. No part of the stem, leaves, or root was unusable. Medicines, food, even poisons, but no time for beauty.

"It would be a good idea to ingratiate

yourself with me," Roland whispered, his eyes stopping on my neckline as he scanned me up and down. "It would be a shame to see you... indisposed again."

Before I could answer he had spun away leaving me in a dreamworld of thorns and branches and for the first time in my life, roses.

# CHAPTER XI

I couldn't help but wonder if Roland knew something. About the girl? About the viciousness of my father's tongue? There was something that made him single me out from the pack. The roses seemed to drift towards me, I gently clipped off a few heads and looked around. This must once have been a lab similar to my own before the plants took over. I could barely make out the counter and gardening stations, the trees and shrubs had grown through the entire room. I managed to push aside a few branches to see a table underneath. Behind me there was a loud crash and I turned to see one of the Guards drop a box of equipment in the doorway.

"Tops' sent you a supervisor, arrives to-night," he grunted.

The doors crashed closed behind him, leaving me inside a room filled with a humid silence and what could very well be a collection of killer plants. I hadn't done a lot of work with these types of plants, propagation and cloning usually happened easily between food crops but flowers...I had no idea if they behaved the same way, if they were structured the same. Or if it was even possible to regenerate the blooms from a single rose bush.

As the night encroached upon the greenhouses and I had no light to work by, the Guard outside opened the door and led me to the line of workers and I saw several faces flick towards me, frowns and anger darkened their faces.

"Looks like Roland's got a new favourite," one whispered to me as she passed. "Is that how you got the cushy gig? Screwing your way through the guards?" The woman, who I barely recognized had a red scar across her face, and I remembered the story Uma had told me of the crop girl who had been branded for treason. Something about smuggling tobacco to the barracks. A flush brushed against my cheek as she whipped past me. They all thought I had slept with the Guard, and now was in some kind of top position. *If only,* I thought to myself as we were shunted out the door.

The journey home was spent in silence, although as we made our way through the forest, a foot slid between mine and I landed face first in the first, spluttering as a sharp pain rocketed through my shoulder.

"Up," the Guard shouted, barely looking back.

The girl who had spoken to me earlier smirked as she passed me in a pile on the ground. I clambered back to my feet and hurried as much as I could with the pain in my ankle. At the house, the Guard barely looked at me as I entered, continuing to take the rest of the girls to the barracks. They'd never been particularly happy that I was allowed the freedom of living away from the concrete, windowless rooms that most of the island inhabited. Little did they know I would have taken a jail cell over living in the dusty memory of my brother and the alcoholic stench of an abusive father.

The house smelt cold, and the sting of whisky had aired out; my father wasn't home. I hurried upstairs to Kimbr, who was still lounging across the soft mattress we had set up, a scattering of books sitting around her. When she saw me, she scowled and picked up an empty bottle.

"I haven't even been able to piss today. Old man only just left," she said, agitated.

I rummaged around in the kitchen for any remnants of food. We were given the same rations as everyone else, but my father often opted instead for a rum or whiskey and despair for dinner, and I found a square of bread wrapped in a towel. After cutting some mould off a chunk of cheese, I reclimbed the stairs and gave it to Kimbr, who grunted a thanks. I sat beside her and let my hand run across the pages of the books. If Roland thought he was going to break me with an impossible task, he was sorely mistaken.

"What are you reading that nonsense for?" Kimbr asked, pulling the book out of my hands and flicking to the back page where a small hollow revealed a box of tobacco.

"I'm a Botanist," I replied. "I like flowers."

Kimbr shrugged, took the tobacco from the book and threw the book itself back to me.

"Righto, consider it yours."

# CHAPTER X

It was a habit now, to run my fingers across the rapidly scarring stripes that the Guards had slashed into my back weeks before. The bristling of rage I usually felt at the thought of the whip had mellowed by then. Somehow, the arrival of Kimbr felt like a pair of arms was coaxing me away from the only life I had known. She was a reminder that the world was so much bigger than what I knew. Every waking minute since I saw her form heaving on the beach, my mind went back and forth. I knew what was out there was awful, worse than here. But there was a chance that far beyond the warming seas and dying land, something better lay. I shook myself and shoved the thoughts back inside. But no one left the island. Not anymore. Especially not those with reproductive capacities. Oh no, the Republic couldn't very well have a hoard of fertile women running around repopulating willy-nilly.

"Who's this?" Kimbr asked, pulling me out of my angering daydream. It was a family picture.

"That's Ace. My brother," I replied, my voice hardening.

"Where is he now?"

"When he turned eighteen he joined the Republican Corps. Haven't seen him since." Kimbr looked me over, a strange look in her eye. "Why not?"

"My father...they never really got along."

"Can't imagine why, he seems like a fabulous man," she said, rolling her eyes.

"Yeah, well...he's all I have left," I answered, the words tasting hollow and ashy in my mouth.

"Have you ever thought of leaving?" Kimbr asked, busying herself searching through the cupboards.

I blinked at her. "Are you serious?"

"Uh...yeah…"

"No one leaves The Island," was all I could think to say. Of course, I had thought of leaving, as a child I had dreamed of it, all the other things the world must surely have held.

"Maybe they should," Kimbr replied, nonchalantly.

I shook my head. "It's not so easy."

"What's stopping you? Really?"

"Well, mostly the Guards, the constant surveillance, my father...and the fact that it's illegal to breathe a word against the Republic."

Kimbr made a 'pfft' sound and waved a hand without looking at me.

"So, you haven't even tried? No wonder you people are all still so trodden on. No one has the balls to rebel against a butterfly, never mind the Republic."

Suddenly irritated, I snapped back at her. "Do you think I don't want to? We're born to do the things we do. I was raised to be a Botanist since I was 15, now I'll work on the plants and Lab until I die. That's just what happens."

Kimbr turned and sighed. "But why?"

I blinked.

"Why what?"

"Why is it that way? Why does everyone on these islands sink to their knees and lap up all the bullshit they feed you?"

A deep swooping cracked in my belly, and I felt tears begin to well in my eyes. I wished I could be like Kimbr or Mae, to believe there's something bigger, something better than the Island and what it held.

Kimbr shrugged. "Hey, I didn't grow up here," she said, softer this time. "It must be hard being raised with all the rules, all the mandates. I'm sorry."

I turned away, wiping my eyes. I didn't even know why I was upset. I had daydreamed of the miracles it would take to get me off this island. Thought constantly as a teenager about what else could possibly be out there. Spend the years mulling about why we spent our lives untangling red tape, working to quotas, obeying the faceless Republic. The possibility of a saviour had been so remote, but now there was a living, breathing example of a dissenter and she was more alive than I had ever been.

"I would kill to leave," I said quietly, not sure if Kimbr could even hear me. It was the first time I had ever said anything like that out loud and I half expected an army of Guards to burst through the door and arrest me for treason. As the dust remained silent, I allowed my shoulders to relax and a few tears to fall. Shaking myself, I sat at the table beside Kimbr and let my fingers run across the gardening book.

"You should make sure that's hidden," she said, quietly. She was avoiding my eyes. "I... I know it's difficult living here. Well, living anywhere these days. But if you want out...you should fight for it."

And die in the process, I thought to myself. But would that be so bad?

# CHAPTER XI

Later that evening, my father stumbled through the door, shaking off his boots and coat, grunting. He was never particularly fond of me but since I had been whipped, we had barely exchanged two words. Not that I minded. I was just about to head upstairs again when there was a pounding on the door. Strange. Before I could see where Kimbr was, the hinges of the door creaked and a thud, thud against the wood forced it open against the lock. Three dark figures stood in the doorway, lamps held aloft, screams billowing through the room.

"On the ground, now!"

In the light of their lamps, I saw a gun glint and the bodies piled into the room. A hand shoved my back and suddenly I was forced flat against the musty carpet, a heavy boot wedging itself between my shoulders. The other figures knocked chairs and plate to the floor as they stampeded up the stairs. With nothing in my line of vision except the yellowing fibres of the carpet in my nose, I froze. They knew! Of course, they knew. How could I have been so careless? I steadied myself, ready for their hands to lift me and take me away. But there were voices upstairs. Arguing. Then silence. Thundering footsteps brought the figures back downstairs as the foot on my back removed itself. Two hands hauled me up. Looking around wildly I took in the situation. My father was being led through the kitchen by two Guards, his arms at his sides, a cut above his eye was bleeding. The room spun.

"What the hell is going on?" I managed to splutter, the Guard behind me grabbed one of my shoulders and when I saw his face, I felt a frozen stone in drop into my belly. I recognized the face that sneered down at me. My brother.

Happy with their prize, the Guards had not entered the attic and I felt relief blow through me when I realized they had not found Kimbr. But why had they taken my father? My father was a horrible man, but he was always loyal to the Republic. Loyal to a fault. Ace stood over me, a blank expression on his face as I took him in.

"Hello, sister."

His voice was thick, gravelly. His face was hidden by a beard, and he was far from the smooth-faced, smiling boy that had left all those years before. I could only stand there and shake my head.

"What are you doing here?"

He offered a half-smile and indicated at

their father's retreating back. "I'm being post-ed here for a while. We are interrogating the Guards who allowed a stowaway to escape custody and remain at large on the island. There are reports our father has been exchang-ing favours for whiskey."

"Reports?"

"Evidence," Ace corrected himself, stick-ing out his chin. "He was seen trading rations for alcohol."

"Really? The man who whipped his own daughter because she didn't reach quota, who let his own wife die a drawn-out painful death instead of offering her any relief...that man was working against his much-loved country? Do you really believe that?"

I took a deep breath as the thought washed over me. Had my father really been so callous? Our rations had become increasingly small of late. But surely not. There was no way…

"Valrye," Ace's voice softened, his hand reaching out to me. "He whipped you?"

"No but he was there," I replied sullenly, the anger I didn't realise I was holding onto was threatening to burst through me. I turned away, trying to gather my thoughts.

"Well, he won't be hurting you anymore," Ace whispered, the tears in his voice not showing themselves on his face. He cleared his throat and waited for me to take it all in. Even after all these years, I believed him. My shoulders relaxed, but my eyes wouldn't focus. I sat heavily on a chair and Ace placed a hand on my shoulder. He felt warm. Familiar.

I caught sight of myself in a mirror and excused myself to clean up. In the bathroom, I steadied my hands against the sink. Taking a deep breath, I splashed a little water on my face, the salt stinging my eyes. When I returned, my mind was still trying to comprehend what I was seeing; my brother in the haphazard living room that had barely changed since he was last in it.

Ace was standing over the fireplace, looking at the photograph that sat above it. It was the same photo that I kept in my work apron, back from the days when the technology to create such things as photographs was still available to the higher-ups. He shook his head from his daydream and turned back to me.

"How long are you staying?" I asked, placing a kettle on the coal range and digging through the overturned kitchen for some tea leaves.

"Republic are posting me here for a while, to oversee the induction of some new Guards."

"Where have you been? It's…been a long time." I felt the muscles in my legs quiver, and I sat down, still trying to move the cold boulder that had settled into my core.

"The Corps are posted around the area. I've been a few places."

"So, there are other things out there?" I asked, something inside me begging for him to at least be happy. Instead, Ace ran his fingers through his hair and clenched his jaw in the way that he always had, and it was like he never left.

"There are. Not places you'd want to go."

I sat silent for a moment, the tumble of thoughts that used to run through my mind returned.

"For a long time after you left, I was…angry. But I always hoped you found somewhere that was better, I guess." I could feel the welling of tears in the back of my throat. Ace didn't look at me but bowed his head. I saw a maze of thick white scars running along the back of his neck and I couldn't help but gasp. Ace quickly turned up the collar of his coat and cleared his throat.

"I'm absolutely shattered, do you mind if we have a real catch up in the morning?"

I nodded, trying not to panic, and smiled as best I could as I thought of the secrets that had developed within our walls since Ace had left.

I could hear Ace snoring through the thin

walls, and I prayed that Kimbr knew to keep as quiet as possible above him. I tried my best to calm the panic that was rising, but it consumed me as I lay there, eventually giving up and sneaking past Ace's sleeping form and pulling the attic ladder down.

# CHAPTER XII

"What the hell's going on?" Kimbr asked in a furious whisper when I had finally re-appeared in the attic.

"My brother is here," was all I could think to say. Not that that explained the depth of shit we were now in.

"Ok," Kimbr said, slowly. "So?"

"So, he's arrested my father. For treason, and he's here to train a whole new batch of Guards. Apparently, they're not overly happy that the current set haven't managed to find you yet."

Kimbr took a breath, peering down the stairs.

"Ok."

"Ok what?"

"I'll go," she said, packing up the piles of junk she had accumulated around her and beginning to pack it back into the case.

"What? Go where? You need to stay here until Mae gets back. You can't just wander around the island."

"So, I should stay here, under the same roof as someone who was sent here specifically to kill me?"

"You stayed while my father was here."

"But he wasn't sober enough to catch the clap."

As she calmly placed the books, tobacco and bottles back into the bag, my hands began to flutter at my sides. Kimbr's arrival had jolted me from a lazy sleep I never realized I was in. She stood before me, unafraid, unforgiving, and I desperately wanted to be the same. To be something more.

"What am I supposed to do now?" I had no idea how to smooth the jumble of my thoughts.

"Whatever you want," Kimbr said, exasperation clear in her voice. "Look, you've lived an average life. You've worked an average job, a cog in the machine, another pair of hands. You're replaceable to these people, nothing special. So, you can either stay here, forget you ever saw me, or you can do something else. Something that actually matters."

The clothes I had lent Kimbr were slightly too big, and her shoulders threatened to escape the loosened seams of the green coat. Her eyebrows raised, waiting for my answer. Before I could even think about it, the words flowed out in a sob. "Where are we going?"

In the end, Kimbr decided bribing the sisterhood was her best option. And so once again, I found myself shivering in the darkness in a strange and unfamiliar place. I was exhausted and sore, I just wanted to collapse into my own bed, stretch out the cramping in my calves. Thoughts of Ace and my father forced their way, uninvited, into my exhausted mind. Had my father really broken the rules? Shaking away the guilt I couldn't explain, I waited. Kimbr had forged on ahead, in an attempt to coax some help from her contact in the Sisterhood. I was too tired to argue and simply sat back, keeping watch. From here I could see two of the three guard towers in this island, the gravelly path a few feet ahead would warn me of incoming enemies.

I was beginning to wonder if I had made the right choice. I could easily be at home, sat in front of the fire, reminiscing with my brother and ingratiating myself to what might be one of the most powerful people in my orbit. Before I could turn around, I heard the crunch of boots and voices.

"We've searched the entire island, where

else could they be?"

"I'm telling ya, this is just a wild goose chase. Bet it's some kind of test."

Their boots almost crushed my fingers, I held my breath, my back pressed uncomfortably against a tree trunk.

"I need to take a leak," one grunted and his boots stopped uncomfortably close to me. A few seconds later, I heard him rezip and trundle on.

As Kimbr insisted on going ahead, I had squeezed myself between two thick branches and disappeared behind soggy mosses. I emerged, irritated, both by what I had heard and the moisture that had soaked through my dress, my skin shivering.

"What took you so long," I whispered furiously when she returned.

"Guards. What's your problem?"

"Nothing, can we just go now?" I asked, collecting the bag of contraband from where I had stashed it.

"They're waiting for us," she whispered, grabbing me by the arm.

"Are you sure they're not just going to kill us?"

"Not yet, I told them we would make it worth their while if they helped us."

We walked slowly, backtracking every few minutes to make following us difficult. Just as I thought we were well and truly lost, we emerged near the run-down barn. The moon was clearer tonight, and I could see that it was an open field area, tall grasses growing around the edge and in the centre wire fences separated the different fields. One of the crop-harvesting stations. I was not completely convinced this was a good idea, but it was all we had. We squeezed ourselves into the hidden door and climbed down through the darkness, eventually emerging in a room of sorts. It was a large open area; the roof was a few tarps that had been nailed to boards. Remarkably it was keeping the place dry. As my eyes adjusted to the dimness, I saw there were half a dozen women seated around a small fire, all armed with large bats, a bow and arrow and even what looked like a spear gun. All pointed directly at us.

# CHAPTER XIII

"At ease," one of the women said, although she looked anything but. Her voice sounded familiar, but a dark hood was covering her face.

She motioned to us to sit, and we gratefully collapsed onto what felt like a termite-eaten trees stump. Waiting for the feeling to come back into my legs I looked around at the faces lit by fire. A few I recognized from the lab, but most were strangers.

The woman pushed back her hood and I looked up to see a very familiar face brooding at me.

"It had better be pretty damn good after last time."

The voice belonged to Uma, and she was not happy. Standing with her arms crossed, her frown lines were deeper than I'd ever seen them. I felt a dizziness overcome me and I felt my breath catch in my throat. What was she doing there? I had never seen her so much as pocket an extra spearmint leaf.

"We have information," Kimbr offered, rummaging around in the backpack. She pulled out the papers I had stolen from the lab, but I already knew they would be next to useless. Uma would already have any information I could offer about the lab. I racked my brain trying to think of what I could offer them. What was valuable? Uma rifled through the papers unimpressed. She rounded on me. "Really Valrye? You really want to dip your toe into this pond? You've no idea how the rest of us grew up here, with your fancy house and your guard father..."

I swallowed, heat rushing through my cheeks.

Kimbr spoke up. "We're all as dead as each other if anyone finds us here so maybe we should cut the bullshit."

A murmur ran through the room and a grumble of acceptance and Uma held up a hand.

"Enough. What has Roland got you working on in your secret lab?"

"Oh, it's nothing important, just busy work. He wants me to regenerate the roses that used to grow a hundred years ago."

"Roses?"

"Yes, I think he just wants me to fail so he can have me arrested," I said, making a face.

Uma frowned, before rushing to the back of the room and grabbing a book from under a mattress. Pulling a single, torn and dirty sheet of paper out she held it up and stared at me.

"What is it?" I asked, not sure if I wanted to know the answer.

"Roses, you're sure?" Uma's eyes widened.

I nodded, confusion replacing the low-level terror. Uma took a deep breath and sat down. She handed me the folder. Flipping it open, I saw it was a scientific plan of some kind. I recognized some of the words but the whole thing made no sense. Large burn holes were torn through it.

"What is it?" I asked again.

"It's plans for a biological weapon. We found scraps of it among the papers, but we never knew what it was. I managed to hide it before we were ransacked."

"A weapon?" Kimbr repeated and a shiver ran through the room.

"It uses a chemical from roses, a poison-very powerful- that can be sent through a populated area and choke the inhabitants to death in mere minutes. When you gave it to us, we assumed the plan had been scrapped since no one's managed to grow roses in over a hundred years."

I tried to steady my hands but every eye in the room was trained on me. A wave of nausea ran through me, and I bent over, head spinning.

"Have you succeeded yet? With the roses I mean," Uma asked.

"Not yet, I thought I had found the problem but...I can't very well succeed now, can I?"

"Ok, ok," Kimbr held up her hands. "We need a better plan that just sitting here arguing. We need to do something; this isn't just theoretical anymore. If we don't stop them, who knows who they'll target."

"Or maybe we should let her grow the fucking flowers, use the weapon ourselves," a young girl spoke up. She couldn't have been more than eighteen.

Uma snapped her head around and for the first time I saw her truly angry. "Don't be so ridiculous! This weapon could kill us all."

The girl grumbled but remained silent.

"We need a better plan than that. This is it; this is what we've been waiting for."

Uma gathered everyone around a make-shift table and soon it was filled with scraps of notes, codes written on everything from sand-wich boxes to pieces of wood ripped off crop crates. Scrawls and doodles sat staring up at me, as though somewhere in the mess was the answer to our problems. We just had to find it.

"How long until they want the rose proj-ect complete?" Uma asked, her voice stronger than I'd ever heard it.

I shook my head, still unable to believe that the rule-obsessed, quota-filling assistant I had known for years had been secretly rebel-ling against everything I thought she stood for.

"Roland said he wants progress by the time Mae arrives. Another week or so, I think. Without a radio, we have no way to communi-cate with her," I spoke, and the words tumbled out, a plan trying to form from my words.

"What about your brother?" Kimbr asked.

"What about him?"

"Will he be a problem?"

I thought for a moment. "Maybe not. We used to be close, I don't think he'd hurt me."

"I hope for your sake that's true. If we can convince the new Guards that they've crushed the resistance, they might give us a little breathing room." Uma's eyes followed me as I stood to leave and I opened my mouth a few times, unsure how to voice everything I wanted to say. Instead, I tucked me head under my hood and stepped back out into the darkness, completely alone this time.

# CHAPTER XIV

As I approached the house, I slipped against the muddy ground and as I fell to my knees, I saw a small pile of soggy feathers clumped together. Kneeling, I saw it was a small sparrow. Strange. Birds weren't common here anymore, nights got too cold. But the tiny thing had a broken wing, and I felt a smile cross my face as I scooped him up into my palm. I took him inside, absolutely no idea what to do with him, and he fluttered against my fingers.

I found him a small bowl of water and let him splash his feathers clean while I made him a nest from raw wool and some old cigar papers. I pressed a soft finger against the back of his head, uncomfortable with the rush of love towards another living thing. Clearing my throat, I saw Ace appear inside.

"Morning," Ace grumbled, dark circles under his eyes. He looked older than he should, I guess in my mind I'd saved him as an angry 18-year-old, floppy hair and a crooked smile. Now he stood here, a man, hunched by the world, or what remained of it. His anger from the night before, whether mellowed or simply dissolved by exhaustion seemed to be gone, even his footsteps were calmer than I recalled.

"Good morning. Would you like some breakfast?" I asked, trying to remain cool. I sat staring at the bird I had placed in the centre of the table.

"I brought some extra supplies with me, wasn't sure if you would have any spare." He lifted his head and did a double-take when he saw the bird.

"You were always too sweet for this place," he muttered with a chuckle as he collected a box out from the laundry room. Fruits I hadn't seen in years spilt out; bananas, guavas, a spiky plant I recognized from a crude painting in the lab as a kiwano. My eyes almost burst from my head as Ace also unloaded several loaves of bread and some dried meat. I hadn't eaten fresh fruit in months, our island rations had been cut time and time again. This was not on the menu. Ace knew how to make me happy, even after twelve years.

"Eat up, I'm going to check in with Roland and maybe I can walk you to work?"

"That would be nice," I said, genuinely smiling. I sat in the watery sunshine with a bowl of fruit listening to the rustle of leaves and felt a strange feeling of peace, my small birdie friend chirping at my side. The pace did not last long. My father's radio sat above the stove, and I heard it burst into life as I finished washing.

"Guard 44Charlie, report in. Over."

Ace's voice sounded in return. "Guard 44Chalie, in. Over"

The sound faded as Ace clomped up the stairs, but I caught a few scraps of the conversation that piqued my interest. "Project Thorn… rebellion…crush." My heart shuddered. They knew. They had found out. How? I tried to shove the feeling down, I wasn't going to help myself by panicking. Deep breath. Ok.

"Normal day," I whispered to myself before Ace returned. He had a strange look on his face, but I had to wonder if it was more the hangover he was clearly nursing.

"Ready!" I said, hitching a smile onto my face.

We walked in silence most of the way, not sure what to say. I had no idea where he had been all these years, how entrenched in the life of a Republic soldier he had become. As we passed the line of crew workers, I saw a few of the women from the night before. I received a few scowls, but no harsh words this time, which I took as a win. Roland was standing at the door as usual, he greeted Ace with a handshake. I entered the Lab, clicking my name badge through the time stamp before pecking Ace a kiss goodbye, still fighting that strange feeling that suddenly my brother was a stranger.

Inside the private lab, I was once again locked inside the rose house, this time with a large delivery of equipment dumped at the door. Rearranging the microscopes, Bunsen burners, heat domes, hydroponics and a collection of shiny things I should probably have no right to ever touch. The Republic must be desperate for these compounds. The roses that already grew were thick and spiky, the flowers half-dead. I imagined that any of the compound that remained in the petals must surely be weak. I needed to work fast to figure out how to clone them. I didn't want to think about what would happen if I failed.

It was around lunchtime when I heard the lab door open. It was Roland. I took a deep breath as he approached, the now-familiar smirk on his face.

"Dare I ask how you are progressing?"

I nodded. "I am getting there."

"Well, we'll see, shall we?" He ran a dirty finger across my forehead, tucking a stray strand of hair behind my ear.

"I know what I need to do now, I just don't have enough hands." Avoiding the shudder that tried to shake down my spine, I forced a meek smile onto my face. "It would go a lot faster if I had an assistant."

Roland looked me up and down. "Assistance, you say?"

"A botany assistant. These plants, in in-experienced hands, can cause a raft of dan-gers-poisoning, warts, rashes...impotence."

Roland took a step back, looking around

in horror. I felt a small tingle and tried to stop my smile as he marched back towards the door. A few minutes later, he returned, Uma following a few steps behind.

Keeping a safe distance beach from my made-up limp-dick flowers, Roland sat himself on a stool directly beside the lab door. I saw Uma's eyes widen as she entered the room, her gaze drifting from the huge walls covered with overgrown ivy vines and palm leaves before dropping on the small wooden garden box in the centre. I had cleared a small path around the roses, and despite all my attempts, it appeared that re-opening the lab had caused their degeneration process to speed up. Still, Uma gasped as she ran a finger across the browning and bruised rose petals. The closest we had ever come to flowers was the time we had bred a hybrid of pineapple sage and a prickly ficus, which produced a strange orange bud that opened to reveal a black peary centre that smelt of burned hair and rotting flesh. I smiled slightly at her face, not having known her to usually be so overwhelmed. As she caught a glimpse of the instruments I had spread across the bench, she shook her head and tutted at me.

"Really? You're using these. I thought you were supposed to be the big, botanist extraordinaire."

Moving quickly, she rearranged my seedlings, and the leafless ivy stalks I was using as a base for the hybrid breeding process. When she was within a few inches of my ear, she whispered in a low voice.

"Do you think this is even possible?"

I sighed. "I didn't think so, but I found the seeds of the apricot plants that died last year. They might work. Not that we can let them ever get their hands on any of it."

Uma nodded slowly, inspecting each of the seeds and sprouts I was working on. We busied ourselves, trying to look hard at work, without actively creating some poisonous super bioweapon.

"Do you have a plan? We can't just fake it forever," Uma whispered to me.

"I know, Roland wants it done by Thursday. Mae's arriving to take the quotas," I replied, my mouth dry and aching. The smell was beginning to give me a headache.

Roland's eyes never left us, we had been working for hours now and he hadn't so much as taken a smoke break or glanced at his watch. Uma was growing increasingly frustrated.

"What is this guy's deal? Do you reckon he knows what the Republic are planning? Does he even care?"

She shook her head, wandering a few minutes before rounding on me.

"Distract him," she whispered.

"What? How?"

"I don't know, but I need his eyes off me."

# CHAPTER XV

My stomach turned at the idea, but I could feel the clock ticking down. Soon, we would be sent home and the lab would be sealed again until tomorrow.

"Fine, but this makes us square," I grunted back at her. I pulled the front of my baggy linen dress down, hoping the strap of my undergarments would be enough to cause a scene. I took a deep breath and wandered back towards the door, eyes on the ground.

"What?" he asked as I approached, eyes still scanning the room.

"I was wondering if you could take me back to the other lab?"

"Why?"

"I need some of the instruments in there, we've almost got it ready to distil the oils from the seeds," I said, clutching at my hands inside my apron pocket so stop them trembling.

"Write a list, I'll send someone."

I took a deep breath. I had absolutely no idea what I was doing, aside from the Guards, there were no men on the island. And I'd never been particularly sad about that. Once boys hit eighteen, they were sent to the Republic army or one of the more exciting islands.

"I was hoping you and I could go...you know...together?" I still had my eyes on the floor but the flush running across my face had now spread to my chest and it felt like an eternity before he answered with a grin that sent the smell of his sickly breath into my nostrils.

In the Lab, I busied myself for a few moments, feeling Roland's eyes on me as I moved. I took a deep breath and turned to him with what I hoped was a smile. He crept closer, his grin widening more than I thought possible.

I placed a hand on his chest. "I need to get the instruments. Those roses are delicate, once it's done…" I offered him a wink and saw his smile shift slightly but he stepped aside and allowed me past. I hoped he couldn't hear the disgust on my voice as I tried to keep up a casual conversation.

Ace was relaxing at the kitchen table when I arrived home, his bare feet propped up on a wobbly stool, cigarette between his lips.

"You don't mind, do you?" he asked when he saw me, waving away the bursts of smoke. Even if I did mind, what could I do about it?

"Not at all. What have you been doing today?"

He seemed strangely relaxed for someone who had just arrested his own father. "Oh, just getting the lay of the land, you know. Seeing how things work around here."

"It's certainly changed a bit," I agreed, boiling the kettle. Would it have been different if he had stayed? I returned to the spindly nest that still sat on the table. The bird's wing, broken, had made it impossible for him to fly away, and he lay, eyes blinking up at me. His breathing was ragged. Two fluffy white feathers sat on the table, and I held my cup of weak tea near the nest to offer some semblance of warmth. His tiny beady eyes stared up at me and I hoped he was glad I was there. Ace watched, sitting in silence as the bird's breathing slowed. Its eyes closed, and I saw his tiny, feathered chest slow and stop. Ace placed a hand on mine, and I felt a thickness in the back of my throat. I shook my head, why was I upset? It was just a bird. Ace scooped it up out of my hands and buried it in a small hole in the garden, while I wiped my, the mug of tea tasting bitter and greasy. When Ace returned, he wrapped an arm around me and squeezed my shoulder. I relaxed into him, and it felt for a moment like he had never left.

"What is it like where they sent you?"

"First, I went to the training facility on Corps Island, it's much like it is here, water and forest but when I was assigned to the corps, we did a travelling tour of the Republic. I saw a lot of islands," his voice trailed off, eyes slipping out of focus. "You should be glad you ended up staying here."

I turned and saw he had stood and was adding kindling to the measly fire I had tried to keep going since this morning. Ace seemed far away, the smoke billowing around him as if it would curl around him and snatch him away.

"Why? What happened out there?

Ace shook his head. "You don't want to know. Truly."

"Hey, you left me here, alone. You're really going to try and tell me that's what was best for me? I was fourteen!"

"I didn't leave you alone, you were with dad."

I shook my head, eyes rolling back automatically as they did at the worst possible times. "Oh yes, thank you so much for that. He was such a fantastic authority figure," I spat out, unable to stop myself.

"He was angry and drunk, all the time when I was here. I was young and stupid. We did nothing but fight, I thought if I left…You were always his favourite." Ace's face had hardened, he was avoiding my eye.

"Well, all that did was re-align his anger. And guess who was the new target?" I spat in anger, immediately wishing to take it back. I felt a swoop of guilt remembering how much I had hated him in those first few years. "I'm sorry. I know you had to leave, I just…wish you'd taken you with me."

He turned to face me; eyes filled with regret. "No, you don't. It's rough out there, the Republic...they run a tight ship. The Islands they control...well, the people on them aren't all as healthy as here."

I sat at the table, running my fingers over the knots that had rotten out of the wood. "Tell me about it," I whispered, pushing the other chair out with my foot.

He sat down, albeit grudgingly and I waited for him to speak but he shook his head. I found a bottle of half-empty whiskey my father kept behind the laundry box. I poured two glasses and waited patiently for Ace to continue his story. He gave me a bit of a distant smile and hesitated before slipping back the whiskey before continuing.

"When I left, I thought it would be tours of the islands, and it was. We went to the Islands who grew cotton, spun wool, made the clothes, but...there are others. Ones they never told us about."

"Did you ever go to the Governing Island?"

Ace nodded, his lips curling into a sneer. "They tell everyone it's the biggest one left these days, but I don't even know if that's true. It's a hierarchy of bullshit to the highest degree. Absolute chaos, everything is wound in red tape, policies for policies sake. Everyone lives freely. No one even really knows where the instructions come down from, we just follow our orders and hope. That's about all anyone can do."

I gulped, shaking. I had spent so much time thinking about how I would escape and despite the fact I knew there was probably nothing better out there, I had always held a tiny piece of silent, unspoken hope. I felt the air deflating from my sails, wondering if the events of the past few days had been worth it. We all wanted off, but where would we go.

"When I was first on patrol, they sent me to the breeding island," Ace continued, though he was no longer addressing me as much as simply talking to himself. "The place they send the women who they call 'good breeding stock', it was disgusting. Do you remember when we took those aptitude exams, you obviously got something suited to you, the whole plant thing, but those who wanted to be mothers, wives...they were picked out specially."

I shuddered, a swirling nausea trying to force its way out. I sipped a little water, hoping to calm my stomach but Ace kept talking, as though spewing out years of crushing trauma was somehow therapeutic.

"There's no face to it!" his fist slammed into the table, sending a crack splitting through it. "There's no one to kill, no one to fight. Nothing that can be changed. It just is," he finished sadly. I sucked in a deep breath. I desperately wanted to spew my guts to him, to tell him everything. Kimbr, the sisterhood, the roses, the books. But I couldn't, not yet. If they thought, he was helping me...Oh God! If I was caught, it wasn't just my own life anymore, I was dragging an innocent man down with me. I felt a nausea that almost dropped me to my knees.

Ace didn't seem to notice. "I'm going to head back to the station, clear my head."

Before I could argue, he was out the door, stumbling slightly as he missed the step.

# CHAPTER XVI

I must have sat shivering for a good hour before I felt like my legs would work again. It was dark now, the moon above cracked like a crystal ball hanging in watch. My brother, a stranger now. What would have happened if he stayed? I had been a toddler when the Republic decided on the segregation, so I'd never really thought about it. Women were the one who made the Botany programme, women were the ones whose labour was free, women were meek, pliable. My father, in a drunken state, had told me how he hand-picked the women that stayed on this island, how when one went down, aged out, died, how he found our 're-placements'. I had shoved it from my mind, but now here it was again, slapping me in the face.

My father's room sat almost exactly as it had for many years. The only new addition now was the large, battered backpack and boots my brother had brought with him. There was a sliver of light shining through the doorway, I almost walked past but something stopped me. I had spent years wishing my brother was home, but now he was here, he was all but a stranger. I pushed the door open completely and wandered inside. I tried to stop myself, the old me would never have considered it, but now… Before he could return, I rifled through the bag, like a hungry gopher. It was mostly clothes, a few tools and some wooden spoons. I shook my head, guilt overtaking curiosity and crammed everything back into the bag. Just as

I was about to leave, something heavy fell on my foot. Annoyance rose over the pain, and I saw it was a solar radio. It was black, heavy, like the ones the Guards used to communicate with the main island. It was drilled into us from childhood that communications between islands were only to be handled by the highest-ranking officer on every island. Why did my brother have one? There were small buttons covering the side, and every fibre of my being wanted to push the call button, hoping that somehow it would connect to Mae, but I knew that would never happen. I had no idea how to reach her, but this was the closest I had ever come. I stood rooted to the floor, unsure which direction to turn.

I crept from the house, leaving a pillow stuffed under my blanket in case Ace returned. The path outside was slippery from the rain but I held steady footing as I made my way to the forestry, trying desperately to find my way in the dark. The bunker the sisterhood gathered in was somewhere deep in the bowels of the island, it had to be. Great way to hide from the Guards, difficult for me to find for a second time. I lost track of how long it took but eventually I saw the shimmer of flame from a grove ahead and recognized the hidden doorway. Before I could reach it, two figures emerged from the trees, a knife suddenly cutting into my throat. After a few moments, the knife lowered, and someone shoved me in the small of the back.

"Inside before they see you. Do you want us all to get caught?"

The room was empty today, Uma and Kimbr were the only ones sat in the dim grunginess.

"What are you doing here?" Uma asked, checking through the thin barred slat of window for anyone who had followed me.

"I found something in my brother's stuff," I replied, breathlessly. Exhaustion was beginning to take over and I realized how long it had been since I had slept properly.

Collapsing onto the chair, I handed Uma the cloth-wrapped radio. Her eyes widened as the handkerchief fell away. She placed it in the middle of the table and stood staring at it, as if it might bite her. She opened her mouth a few times, but eventually settled on silence, running a hand through her hair.

"Do you know how to use it?" Kimbr eventually asked and I shook my head, realising that maybe it wasn't so useful after all. I picked it up, turning it over in my hand. The buttons and knobs on the top twisted under my fingers and the crackle of static boomed through the room. Twisting the knob as I had seen my father do a few times. The crackle slipped in and out, until an inaudible grainy voice sounded. Uma gasped, shaking her head and reached into her pocket and pulled out a few of the crushed rose petals she had managed to collect from the Lab while Roland was preoccupied. Placing them on the table alongside the radio and the scraps of paper holding fragments of information, we stared at the pitiful collection. It was all we had to show for...everything. But it was more than I could have imagined.

"Is it enough?" I whispered to Uma. "To buy us good faith with another island?" Uma shrugged. "I honestly don't know, but I've been waiting for years for something to happen and ...this is the furthest we've ever got. It must be enough. It has to."

As the sun rose through the gunmetal clouds, I heard Ace thumping around and I held my breath. As soon as he discovered the radio was missing, he would know I took it. But I was ready. If I needed to be punished to get those girls out of here, I could take more lashings. I dithered as much as I could before emerging from my room for breakfast. Ace nodded a good morning to me, his face strained but he didn't say anything, just looked at me strangely for a moment.

"I have to get going," he said, his eyes glistening. "I'm helping train some new Guards this morning. Maybe we could have dinner later?" his voice had changed, there was a sadness in it now.

"That would be nice." A smile spread across my face. I wondered if he had noticed the missing radio. His eyes lingered, about to say something when there was a knock at the door. Roland's frame was crammed into the doorframe, large and leering. He offered me a wink and a crude sneer before addressing Ace.

"Ready to go?"

"Yes, I am, I could have made my own way there," Ace replied, looking slightly annoyed at the interruption.

"I thought after the state you were in last night that you might need some help finding your way to some hair of the dog."

# CHAPTER XVII

The Lab felt hot and constricting as I worked. I had always found plants freeing, the wafting of trees and leaves soothing but today as we worked in the heat, I just wanted to rip my work-apron off and run for the ocean. At least Mae was due to arrive within the next few days. I just had to hold on a little longer…

"Chop, chop," Uma's irritated voice came from behind me. "It's not going to grow itself." I told myself she was only putting on a show for the Guards, but I knew she just enjoyed bossing me around after I had almost gotten them all caught.

"Kimbr is gathering everyone up," she muttered under her breath. "We'll be ready to go when Mae arrives."

I nodded, still unsure that our half-cooked plan would work. "How are we going to get everyone on board?"

"Don't worry about it, you just be ready unless you want to be left behind."

I took a deep breath, trying to hold back the stinging feeling in the back of my throat. I was starting to have doubts, fears. I finally had my brother back. I had stayed awake most of the night trying to convince myself that was enough of a reason to stay but I also knew I couldn't. None of us could. If I stayed behind, we would be detained and questioned, anyone left behind would be tortured for information. I had seen it all before. I shook off the feeling, focusing instead on the seedlings in front of me. I had successfully managed to merge two varieties of almond sapling, the closest living plant to the rose.

"How much do you reckon they know about plants?" I asked Uma, glancing at the Guards at the door. There were two of them today, both bored looking, and Roland was nowhere to be seen.

"Doubt they know much of anything," she replied dryly.

"So how would they know if we've succeeded?" Uma looked around, nodding slowly. "That...is a very good point. That's your bargaining chip. Use it if we get caught."

Great, I thought. Even Uma thought we didn't have much of a chance. Once the Guards had looked away, she gripped me by the shoulders.

"I mean it. If we get caught. You scream and fight and keep yourself alive, you hear me? You're the best this island's ever seen, that's why you're the only one who can give them what they want." Her voice was rough but there were tears forming in the creases of her eyes. Clearing her throat, she turned back to the flowers, running a hand along them. "At least if I die trying to get out of here, I can say I've seen a rose. Not many can say that."

I imagined Kimbr sheltered in the bunker, gathering the meagre supplies she could get her hands on and waiting. Waiting. When Ace arrived home, he found me at the window, peering down at the tatty jetty. No sign of Mae's boat and the sun was about to go down. Ace sat heavily at the table, shaking off his boots in the same way our father used to. He looked tired. Just like our father.

"I saw our father today," he said, as if he knew what I was thinking. My heart leapt into my throat, where it resided more and more often these days.

"What? Why?"

"The Guards...have to let him go. Those at the top decided there wasn't enough proof to charge a high-ranking Guard. Not when we're so low on men as it is."

He sighed, rubbing his forehead.

"Did he say anything?" I felt strange, the thought that he was sitting in some prison somewhere.

"He claimed he was trading information, but no one saw him. He confessed but they're punishing him with relocation."

"Information?"

"Mmm hmm, bunch of papers went missing from the labs."

My stomach clenched at his words. He confessed? Had he known it was me? I turned away so Ace wouldn't see my face and busied myself over the kettle.

"Where is he now?" I asked softly, my mind whirring. Papers? I kept repeating to myself. The papers from the lab? Had my father taken the blame?

"He's being relocated. You won't have to worry about him anymore. But that means you'll have to move into the barracks. They won't have you staying here alone," he whispered the last part barely looking at me.

"But he's gone now, can't you stay? Please?" my voice cracked a little and I tried to cover it with a cough. Ace wasn't fooled and carefully took hold of my arms and pressed me into his chest. I felt him sigh.

"I can't. Not after everything that's happened. Not everyone knew what he was like. He still has a lot of friends here."

I let out a breath I didn't know I was holding and poured myself a drink, forgetting for a moment about Mae and the boat. My voice stiffened. "When are you leaving?"

"I don't know, but soon."

I sat back in my chair, the silence thickening between us. I felt tears rising but I pushed them down. I had already grieved my brother; I had already lost him. This was just a time-out from the loneliness. Plus, he was just something else the Guards could use against me if I was caught. Better for everyone if we both got out of here. I wandered back to the window and saw that lamps on the dock had been lit.

"Mae's boat is due in tonight," Ace said, and I turned to him in surprise. He smiled "You two were always close, even as kids. I assume she stays with you when she visits. How did you manage that?" I smiled a little. "Dad organized it once, he'd had a bit to drink so he let it slide. No one ever argued," I remembered.

Ace nodded, pointing out the window. "Speak of the devil."

Mae's boat, bobbing slightly juddered up to the beach in the distance.

"I'll leave you to it," Ace said, heading for the stairs.

"No, wait. Don't you want to have dinner?"

He sighed, suddenly looking older that he should. "I'm tired, I might just turn in. Say hi to Mae from me. I really am sorry I left you," he whispered.

"I know." I couldn't help but pull him into another hug. Not wanting him to let go, I felt the guilt weighing me down. I almost opened my mouth, told him everything. But I couldn't risk Kimbr and Uma, Mae and the others. I simply smiled and nodded as he disappeared up the stairs.

# CHAPTER XVIII

Mae arrived at the door, her face was shad-owed and seemed more creased than usual. As she crossed the threshold, another figure appeared behind her, skulking in on her tail.

"Greetings, Ma'am, I am here to oversee the quota transfer," the man said, barging his way inside and Mae shot me a look of anger and rolled her eyes. My heart began hammering. A Guard on Mae's shadow was not going to make our plan any easier. "The courier here claims this is her place of residence when she stays here, is this correct?"

"It is." I cleared my throat.

"And is there a Guard present for your safety?"

"Indeed, there is. My brother is asleep upstairs. He reports directly to the Republic's top officers," I claimed wildly, no idea if I was speaking the truth or not.

At the mention of Ace, Mae's head snapped around and looked at me, eyes widened. The man with her seemed to be happy enough with my answer and sat himself down at the table.

"Well alright then. Might I trouble you for some dinner. It's a fair trek from Colony."

"If you would be more comfortable at the Guard's barracks, I would be happy to show you the way," I said pointedly.

The man offered me a sly grin. "Oh no need for that. I'm just here to keep this one out of trouble," he said, jerking his head at Mae. My mind racing, I nodded. "Well, I guess welcome to you. I will prepare us some food."

Clattering around in the kitchen as Mae stalked the loungeroom angrily, I found the remnants of our potatoes, beginning to sprout and our wheat cakes that tasted of nothing. Adding a few herbs gave it some flavour and as I was sprinkling rosemary on top, I cast a glance at the table. The new arrival was whistling away to himself happily, his back turned.

"What the hell is going on?" I whispered furiously to Mae, who shook her head.

"I wish I knew. I was about to cast off when ol' Roly over there showed up. Told me he was assisting with the collections this month. Something about a high-priority project for the Republic?" Mae scowled, her voice cracking in anger.

I closed my eyes and sighed. "The roses."

"What?"

"Never mind," I said, shaking my head and pulling her in close. "We have a big problem."

As I whispered furiously to Mae, it occurred to me that she had never explicitly agreed to our plan. Kimbr and Uma had been so certain, but Mae was innocent in all this. We had just assumed she would put her life on the line. Her horrified face as I spoke made my stomach sink.

"I... I'm so sorry! I... we made this plan, I knew it was a shitshow, but I'm desperate. We're all desperate."

Mae placed a hand on mine, smiling and skating her head. "Don't be ridiculous. You know the second you ask me for help, I will do anything for you." She took my hand in her own and rubbed my calloused fingers. For a moment everything froze, and I wished we could stay there, together, forever. I let out a shaky breath. "But what do we do about him?"

Stirring the wheat and rosemary, I had a flash of culinary inspiration. Digging through the herbs I found an old jar of castor bean oil that I had once used as rat poison. It killed rats and offered hallucinogenic but non-fatal effects in humans, I sprinkled it over one of the plates. Hoping the rosemary would cover the taste, I slopped some of the stew into bowls.

At the table, we sat in silence, the large unwelcome man slurping down his dinner as Mae and I sat stiff-backed, pretending to sip the gruel.

"Drink?" I asked the man as he cleaned his bowl with his large, prickled tongue.

"Got anything good?" he asked, chuckling.

"We both know if I did, I would be in some pretty serious trouble, wouldn't I?" "I won't tell if you won't," the man winked.

Pouring a large glass of the thick whiskey, I grabbed some blankets and dumped them into a pile on a thinly slatted bench. As the whiskey and castor bean began to take effect, I saw his eyes droop and he stumbled to his feet.

"Wowsers, that's some strong stuff there missy," he slurred, collapsing to the ground.

"Jesus, I haven't been able to move without him watching," Mae muttered, giving him a kick to the shin and he let out a snore. "Prick."

"Quick, we need to go. Uma is waiting for us."

Holding Mae's clammy hand, we ran into the forest, the tracks under our feet weaving in and out of the undergrowth. I took one last look at the house, at the dark window where Ace was obliviously sleeping. I had put everything out of my mind. One foot at a time. One thing to worry about, one step, one mission. If I stopped, if I thought about Ace, or my father, or everyone that would be left behind to bear the brunt of our actions, I felt I might collapse into nothingness. We reached the bunker with little oxygen left in our lungs and Uma pulled us inside with a scowl.

"Took you long enough," she muttered.

I looked around, expecting half a dozen

women I knew Uma worked with. I gasped aloud as I saw more than twenty women staring back at me, their sad, sunken eyes pleading, desperate. I swallowed, frozen but Mae pushed past me, taking charge.

"We can't all leave at once, we'll move out in threes," she said, nodding to Uma. "Do you have everything?"

There was a murmur of agreement and Kimbr stepped forward, the radio in her hand.

"Ok, we just need to wait for the Guards to change shifts. There are short windows where the boat will be unattended."

The static of the radio crackled and made us all jump.

"Guard base, come in, over."

"Guard Base responding."

"Guard Willace will be examining the stations this evening, over."

"What does that mean?" Kimbr asked, panicked

I put a hand on her shoulder, jerked back

to the reality we were facing. "It's ok, it just means the head Guard is going to be wandering around. But it's good we know."

I sucked in the putrid, musty air that had accumulated in the grimy bunker and braced myself. It was almost time.

"Ok, as soon as the changeover starts, we'll head out." My voice sounded a hell of a lot more confident than I felt. "When you leave, run. Stick to the trees, does everyone know where the grove is? We're meeting there," I spoke in rambling sentences, knowing that if I stopped, the reality of what we were about to do would hit me like a ton of bricks. Already I wasn't sure when the time came if I would be able to move my own stiffening legs.

# CHAPTER XIX

We sat in complete silence, crowded around the radio, waiting. The guards changed shift every 8 hours. They should have radioed in a changeover order by now. I was about to give up, assuming that today after an entire lifetime of strict routine, that whatever God remained up there, decided to play some cruel joke on us. I wasn't sure if it was terror or relief when the radio crackled into life.

"Guard changeover one. Shift three incoming.”

Mae and Kimbr jumped to their feet, herding the first three women, all older, one hobbling with a cane. As they disappeared into the night, I felt a horrible curdling in my stomach. Three more women went. Then another pair. Then it was just me and Kimbr left. The thought that I had sent these women to their deaths coursed over me, but before I could do anything I felt Kimbr's hand push me out the doorway and grip my elbow. Before I knew it, I was running, my feet slipping against the mossy ground, blindly searching for Mae and Uma and finding only darkness.

The trip between the bunker and the grove was not far, it took only a few minutes and the last of us made it just as the radio sprung to life again. Catching my breath, I looked around, counting. Where was Mae?

"Mae?" I whispered desperately, but Kimbr shoved me onwards. I saw Mae's dark hair up ahead and spat out the bitter taste in my mouth.

"Quick, we need to go!"

I watched the others passed us, in twos and threes sneak through the trees and towards the only hope of safety they'd seen in a very long time. As the last of the women crept from the bowels of the forest, a figure crashed from the trees behind me. I raised my hands, ready to fight whichever Guard emerged. My heart fell into my stomach as I saw who it was.

"Ace?!"

I motioned for Kimbr to go on without me and she hesitated but continued to run in a low crouch throwing a few looks back at me. Ace spoke slowly, his head shaking before dropping into his hands.

"I figured it was you," he said through his fingers. "I didn't want to believe it...are you really working with the resistance?"

My chest thumped so loud I was surprised I could hear him. "I just sort of...fell into it."

"Val, you need to go back now." His voice

sounded desperate now, he was looking around as if he couldn't believe what was before him. He grabbed my arm. "I'm serious. You need to get back to the house. The guards know! They'll be here any minute!"

My heart sank. "I can't," was all I could whisper as his hands squeezed my arms and an anguished cry left his lips. "I... just can't stay! The lab...they want me to help them build a weapon." The words were coming out jumbled, I knew he didn't understand but he released me anyway.

"A weapon?"

"Something that will kill people. We can't stay, any of us. We can't just wait for something to happen..." I trailed off, tearing at the itchiness in my skin from the sea breeze. "Please...I can't stay, you don't know what it's like here now."

Ace looked once again at the guard booth, then at me. For a moment we were children again, him much larger than me, his protective body shielding me from our father's wrath, his dishevelled and bruised face staring at me as he left the island all those years ago. He wasn't the same brother I knew back then; the Republic had changed him. It had changed me too. He held my hands in silence for a moment before standing aside, hastily wiping his glistening eyes on his sleeve.

"Go. I'll buy you some time."

I tried to force my arms to work, to throw them around him, or to whisper a thank you but he had turned on his heel and disappeared into the forest before I could move. I stood frozen, wondering if I didn't move if it would all go away, if the reset button would appear and I could wake up from the horror show I had found myself in.

"Val!" Kimbr hissed and, barely aware of my flailing limbs I somehow managed to make my way to her side and join the others near the edge of the beach.

We walked as one, a shifting, creaking,

shadow until the sand softened under our feet. I could see the lights of the dock, the swaying of the boat. We were close, so very close. There were several women in front of me, and as I turned to search for Mae, a slicing woosh emerged from the trees. One of the women ahead of me fell to the sand with a scream, before a silver spear whizzed past my face, embedding itself into the ground between Kimbr's feet. Bodies pressed against bodies as we scrambled for cover, an army of figures dressed in black converged on us. I felt crushing, a pain and then...nothing.

# CHAPTER XX

Voices swirled around me, but I kept my eyes tightly shut. We weren't on the beach anymore. It was silent, still. I felt icy cold concrete beneath my body, my crumpled figure was adding pressure to my joints and sending shockwaves of pain through me. I listened, trying to avoid moving the aching limbs I wasn't sure were still attached. Before I could orient myself, I felt two hands grab me but the arms and haul me to my feet. I tried to blink but there was nothing but darkness, something was covering my eyes. I tried to speak but my mouth was bound shut. I could do nothing but panic as I was dragged along the ground, eventually thrown into a chair. I heard a voice and suddenly a blinding light burnt into my eyes as the cloth was ripped off my head. I was in one of the barracks, empty except for a lone figure shadowed against the only lamplight.

"Well, well, it's been much too long." The voice sent a shiver through me. Roland.

I squinted, a wave of nausea overtaking the throbbing in my head, and I learnt as far forward as I could with my arms tied to the chair and felt the hot, burning in my throat as I spat at Roland's feet. His sneer didn't move, he simply brought his face close to mine, his breath stank of blood and whiskey, and I noticed there was a cut above his eye that was seeping into a bruise. His eyes glinted as he glared at me, silent.

"I should have known you'd be involved.

I must say I didn't think you'd have it in you. Running away? Tsk, tsk."

His fingers ran through my hair and as a strand stuck to my face, I realized it was coated with blood.

"Nothing to say? You, my dear, will tell me the truth, the whole truth, the whole plan. Where did you think you could go? You were just going to sail around in a little lover's boat, huh?"

I looked desperately around but there was no one else in the room. I was alone.

"Oh, don't worry," Roland said, cheerfully. "I thought you might be a little shy. So, I brought you some company."

The door behind Roland scraped open and another Guard entered, this time dragging a wailing, kicking Mae. She was gagged as well, but I could tell from the bruises blossoming on the Guard's face she had not come easily.

"Ah, welcome. Just in time."

Mae was thrown into the chair opposite

me, her hands tied with thick ropes as she struggled to break free.

"Mae!" I called out but all that answered me was a fist to the back of the head and the cloth being shoved back into my mouth.

I screamed against the gag, my mouth feeling the fabric ripping into my lips. I felt that if I hadn't been tied to the chair, I would collapse into a pile of nothingness. The hollow in my stomach flowed to my limbs and I felt like the remnants of a seashell washed onto a beach of death. My vision blurred as Roland and another of the guards dragged Mae's chair directly in front of me, so close our knees almost touched. My mouth gummy and dry, I tried to speak against the gag, but Roland patted me on the head.

"Now, now, you've had your chance. We'll let this one have a turn."

His footsteps disappeared behind me, and I couldn't see anything but Mae, whose eyes were wide and pleading, as if trying to tell me something. Time slowed, sound ceased to make sense and as Roland emerged from the darkness, he held in his fist a rusted hammer and a rope. With every muscle in my body struggling against my bonds, I lurched forward, the concrete ground all I saw before I was once again thrown into nothingness.

I tasted blood in my mouth before I realized I was conscious again. I wondered for a moment if I was dead, or at least in the process of dying but the pain ripping apart my skull pulled me back to the dingy barracks of The Island. I was flat on my back, someone had pulled a thin blanket up to my chin and propped my head up, which was succeeding only in allowing the blood to run down my throat. With a cough, I struggled to sit upright, taking in the room around me. Around every wall, bruised and shivering women sat, deathly still and huddling together.

# CHAPTER XXI

The silence was unnerving, and although my head felt as though my skull had been forced into several pieces, any complaints caught in my throat when I saw everyone else. Uma sat near the doorway, her back to me and when I tried to stand, she turned, revealing burns across the side of her face, her hair charred to cinders from her forehead to her shoulder. I reached out a hand, but she turned away, and I saw she was focused on Kimbr, who lay next to her, unmoving.

"Kimbr?" I whispered as I moved closer, trying to avoid the pain in my limbs.

Uma held up a finger to her lips in a *shhh* motion and peered through the crack in the door. I made my way through the room of broken bodies and sat beside her. Kimbr was breathing but only just, and I saw she had cuts running deep into her back, much worse than any lashing I had ever seen before, and I shuddered.

There was a resignation in the room, it cascaded over me like a toxic wave, and I saw everyone that had before now stood tall and determined crouched in defensiveness. Mae was nowhere to be seen.

"Have you seen Mae?" I whispered to Uma but before she could answer there were footsteps outside the door, and she pushed me to the ground and covered me with a blanket.

"Close your eyes!" she demanded in a furious whisper, and I obeyed, sure the pounding in my chest would betray me to anyone who entered.

There was the scraping of a key, and the door opened a tiny sliver. An eye appeared in the gap before the room was flooded with watery light. Ace. His eyes were both black, his arm hung uselessly at his side, and I smelt a stomach-turning aroma of burning flesh, but he threw the door open, a large duffel bag in his hands.

"It was all I could find," he spoke slowly, spitting a mouthful of blood on the ground. He placed the bag at the entrance to the door. No one moved, their eyes turning to me. I stood, my mouth opening and closing, my mind refusing to form a cohesive thought. After a second, I nodded at them.

"It's ok, we can trust him."

He nodded to me, and I tried to smile a thank you back, but the door slammed closed, and he retreated outside. Uma opened the bag, exposing ragged bandages, cloths, sheets and a few hastily gathered herbs from the medical hut. I dug through them, desperately hopeful. There were a few dried kawakawa leaves and as I moved aside some of the scattered debris, I saw a final piece of tissue. As I lifted it out, it unravelled and three delicate rose petals fell into my hand, all beginning to crinkle at the edge, the scent soft and beautiful in a room full of destruction. Ace had made good on his word. Even though we had been captured, I felt a strange sort of peace at the knowledge that the biological weapon they had planned was, at least for now, incomplete. I smiled and tucked them into my pocket, before taking the leaves and crushing them between my fingers.

Looking around, the barracks were bare, but in the bathroom, there was a small amount of water remaining in the sink. There was just enough in it to make the leaves into a poultice, and I smeared it through my fingers, despair threatening to overtake me. There was no way there were enough bandages or herbs for everyone, who needed it the most? I knew I didn't have long to decide, if Roland or any of the other Guards returned and saw them, they would be confiscated. Kimbr on the floor appeared to be the most urgent. She had regained consciousness, but barely. Her head was moving side to side, her eyes remained closed. Through my work growing medicinal plants, I had some experience of medical applications, but I was far from an expert. I swallowed, the threat of death hung heavy in the room, and they were all looking at me. I slathered the pulp onto Kimbr's shoulder, dressing it as best I could. Uma was my next concern, though I had no idea how my concoction would work on burns. She waved my hands away, but exhaustion coaxed her down and I rubbed the poultice onto her face. I couldn't bandage it, so I had to leave it to burn in the salty air. She grunted but didn't complain. None of them did. None of them said anything.

Night fell before the door opened again,

this time a figure draped in black rags was tossed inside, groaning. Pulling aside the hood, I saw it was Mae. My heart dropped through the bottom of my stomach, as I saw her face. The face I had known since childhood was burned, cut and bruised but her eyes were open, and they were spitting fire.

"Oh my god," I whispered as she tried to stand, her weight falling against me. I held her warmth in my arms and helped her to the closest bed. Cradling her head against my shoulder, I heard her whisper into my chest.

"I'm going to kill him."

The night darkened the thin windows that lined the barracks, the women did not move, as if they had been frozen in hopelessness. Kimbr had woken a little more and was now pacing the room, slamming her fists into the bars that covered the door and windows.

"It's no use," Uma snapped.

Kimbr sat, angrily, her feet twitching. I felt exhaustion dragging my eyelids closed but

I forced them open again, I couldn't afford to let me guard down. None of us could. We heard nothing more from the guards, every now and then, one would peer through the window or door, ensuring none of us had died. But we were left on our own. I stood every hour or two, checking on the others for no other reason that I was unable to do nothing. Kimbr was beginning to spike a fever but refused the compress I had fashioned from a ripped tunic and cold water. I was about to force it onto her injuries anyway when there were footsteps outside the door again. The women automatically crowded away from it, attempting to shelter each other from sight. I heard a familiar cough, a sigh then the turning of a key. As the door was inched open, my father stood before me, his face battered but, in his hand, he held a spear gun. He looked at me, and when his eyes rested on my bruised face, he let out a sob and dropped his head into his hands.

"I'm sorry," he whispered to me, glancing

left and right. "I'm so sorry." He swung the door open and motioned for us to follow him. I didn't move, sure it was a trap.

"What are you doing?"

"Apologising…Look I'm sorry about, well, all of it." He shuffled, flustered.

"Bit late now,'" was all I could say. I shouldn't be questioning any chance of help.

"Yeah…forced sobriety will do that." I saw his eyes slick with tears, his hands trembling.

"You took the blame for me?" I had never trusted my father to bring home the weekly rations, never mind break me out of prison, but as his strangely sober eyes pleaded with me, I nodded to the women to stand.

"Please, I know I have not done enough for you. Let me do this now. I reported another escape attempt on the other side of the island. You have to go now, or you'll never get out of here alive. Go!" His voice quivered, and I saw he was using the spear gun to hold himself upright. He looked barely alive. Uma stood and looked him up and down before helping Kimbr to her feet.

"We need to go. Now. To the beach."

"There are Guards posted at the dock. Two of them. You'll need this," he said, handing me the weapon.

"What about you?"

"I'm done. I won't make it. You must go," he said, matter-of-factly handing one of the women a bag. "There's some rations in there, not much, but it's better than nothing."

"Why are you doing this?" I asked.

"When your mother died, I failed you. I turned into the opposite of what you needed. Your brother...he… well, it doesn't matter now. I can't fix it with him, but I can help you. Please. Go."

# CHAPTER XXII

Once the bedraggled group of women had managed to form a wavering queue, we began the long and deadly walk to the beach. I brought up the rear, looking over my shoulder at my father, who nodded and smiled as best he could with his injuries. I choked back a sigh and almost ran back, but Mae took my hand. We ran. And we didn't stop until we reached the sand, the Guard post in the distance flickering two shadows against the moonlight. Mae's boat remained moored just off the beach. So close.

"Wait here," I whispered to the rest of the group, raising the speargun.

Keeping to the trees I got as close to the guards as possible before revealing myself. I lined up a shot, unsure of how good my aim was. My finger danced against the trigger, and before I could chicken out, I stood to take the shot. Just as my finger was about to shoot, one of the figures turned and a flash of the near-by torch lit up a bruised face. Ace. He saw me a second after I recognized him and he stood, stunned and confused. The other man turned, his hand immediately reaching for his baton but before he could grasp it, Ace had swung his arm around the other man's neck, squeezing. The other Guard collapsed to the ground, and I ran to my brother, throwing my arms around his neck and sobbing.

"How did you get out?" he whispered into my ear.

"Dad," was all I could say, and I collapsed against his chest, clinging on for dear life.

The others emerged from the trees and slowly made their way to the boat ahead. As I let go of Ace, there was shouting from somewhere above. Guards had realized the explosion was a distraction and had returned to find the barracks empty. They were not happy. Red-faced Roland led the charge, galloping down the stone steps towards us. Mae saw him before I did and before I could stop her, she grabbed the speargun out of my hand. A single shot. She aimed. Fired. A shot of thin metal buried itself directly into Roland's chest. I watched him collapse and tumble down the stairs. A thump and he was a crumpled heap, gasping for breath.

"Go, now!" Ace shoved me towards the boat.

"Come with us!" I begged, trying to drag him along the sand. He ran with us for a moment, but we were slow and injured and the Guards were gaining on us. We were only a few steps ahead now and as I reached the boat, Mae grabbed me by the arm and threw me over the side and Ace stood on the rotting wooden jetty.

"Be safe," he called out as Mae shoved me below deck. I fought her, the tears rolling down my cheeks, but Ace had already turned away, his fist catching the nearest Guard in the face. I heard the engine chug to life and the smell of diesel filled my nostrils, making me waver on my feet. The boat shuddered under the weight of the unexpected cargo, but Mae's expert hands guided it out of the cove. I could do nothing except watch as Ace shrunk out of sight.

The Island was all any of us knew, and there was a tense silence as it dwindled from sight, the waters beneath us deep and choppy. Kimbr guided us as best she could from her enforced rest in bed. She told us of Islands where books lined the streets, where Guards were protectors, where plants grew naturally, but I had no idea how much of it was a fever-dream.

"Where do we go from here?" Mae asked Uma who stood frozen in place. She shook her head as the island disappeared into the fog. As children we had often whispered about Freedom Island, of what might be out there. The conversations petered out as we grew old and the realisation that we might never know what was out there hit us. I knew she still clutched onto hope as the rest of us did, but we were fast running out of food, the only water was what was left from Mae's last trip. We wouldn't survive more than another day.

I stood on the deck of the boat that rocked us gently, cradling us to the earth when all I wanted was to disappear into nothingness, to float away. My eyes burned as I kept them open, not daring to blink in case I missed another Navigator vessel or some small evidence of another island nearby. It was almost dark when I saw distant greenery looming over the horizon. Bushed appeared to sprout out of the ocean itself, and as we approached, I saw an inlet that led to a canal.

"I guess that's where we're going," I said, as Mae, Uma and Kimbr stood behind me on the deck, quivering. Darkness had fallen now, but there was no sign of life or light on the island. I could tell by the look on Mae's face she didn't recognise where we were. I turned around and took stock. We were tired, seasick, and desperate. I made the decision.

As we glided through the water, trees crushed down on us from above, small patches of solid ground appeared every now and then until eventually the stern juddered against some undergrowth. I had no choice but to leave the boat and continue foot in the hopes of finding…something, anything. I took a breath, closing my eyes and thinking of Ace. Mae gently held my hand as I took a step up onto the hull. My foot floated above the ground for several seconds before I lowered it to the soft and soggy ground.

The air was cold but the shivers that ran through us had less to do with the weather and more to do with the absolute uncertainty that none of us had ever experienced before. For once in our lives, we were in charge. We were the women they warned us about.

# About the Author

Ashleigh Cattermole-Crump is an author, mother and kitchen witch from New Zealand. She has published many short stories and is the author of a literary cookbook, The Writer's Cookbook.

She received her bachelor's degree from Otago University as well and also has degrees in education and advanced creative writing.

More on her work can be found here:

www.facebook.com/ashcattermolecrump

# More From Nordic Press

**Novels/Novellas**

Face of Fear by C. Marry Hultman
9789198671001

Dawson Junior G3 by Brian Wagstaff
9789198671049

Boy in the Wardrobe by Esther Jacoby
9789198684018

New Life Cottage by Esther Jacoby
9789198671056

The Wait by Esther Jacoby
e-book:https://books2read.com/u/4Dgz8Q

Liebe ist Warten by Esther Jacoby
9789198671070

Das Cottage by Ester Jacoby
978919868407

Musing on Death & Dying by Esther Jacoby
9789198671063

Earth Door by Cye Thomas
9789198671025

An Odd Collection of Tales By Cye Thomes
9789198684124

Graffiti Stories by Nick Gerrard
9789198671018

Punk Novelette by Nick Gerrard
9789198671087

Struggle and Strife by Nick Gerrard
9789198684049

Fake Escape by Natalie Hughes
e-book:https://books2read.com/u/bMXL5X

Hell Hath No Fury by Chisto Healy
9789198750706

True Mates by E.F. Vogel
9789198750713

<u>CHRONICLES</u>

Six Days to Hell by E.L. Giles
9789198684087

Cold as Hell by Neen Cohen
9789198684094

Murder Planet by Adam Carpenter
9789198671032

Generation Ship by Adam Carpenter
9789198684063

Sunshine by L.T. Emery
978-9198750942

MYTHOS
Antisocial Housing by Tim Mendees
978-9198750959

ANTHOLOGIES

Just 13
9789198684025

Lost Lore & Legends
9789198671094

Rise and Fall
9789198750911

Worlds Collide
9789198750928